Buttmen 2

EROTIC STORIES AND TRUE CONFESSIONS BY GAY MEN WHO LOVE BOOTY

Edited by Alan Bell

WEST BEACH BOOKS

Buttmen 2 is a West Beach Book

West Beach Books
PO Box 68406
Indianapolis IN 46268
www.westbeachbooks.com
www.buttmenfunzone.com

Designed by Alan Bell
Copy Editor: Robert Gaylord

First Paperback Edition: May 2002
First Paperback Edition ISBN 1-931875-04-9
ISBN may vary on electronic editions.
LCCN: 2002100829

Cover model: Caesar (www.caesarworld.com)

Buttmen 2

EROTIC STORIES AND TRUE CONFESSIONS
BY GAY MEN WHO LOVE BOOTY

Table
of Contents

A Note About
Safer Sex

*B*uttmen 2: Erotic Stories and True Confessions by Gay Men *Who Love Booty* bears witness to various aspects of men's sexuality as it relates to the male ass. This anthology strives to provide insight into our fantasies and realities by allowing the authors to communicate freely about what they think about and what they do to explore their love of men, ass and sex.

West Beach Books acknowledges that some of the sexual acts within these pages fall outside the current definitions of safer sex. Our intent is not to condone, condemn or judge individuals or individual choice, but rather to present a forum for free expression of sexuality and sexual matters.

We do, however, encourage all Buttmen to educate themselves in all matters of sexual health, to know current medical positions on safer sex, and to take personal responsibility for one's actions with full knowledge and awareness of the potential consequences of those actions.

What Is It About Butt?

MATTHEW STEWARD

What is it about butt that causes so many of us to swoon, drool and lose control of our faculties?

As with many lovers of men, I came to the butt relatively late (it almost seems like a prerequisite to fixate first on the dick). The furtive glances of crotches in the junior high locker room gave me my first clue that I was gay, and soon after, I developed a distinct preference for well-built or muscular forms. Shortly thereafter, I began to deconstruct the bodies themselves—chest, arms, legs and inevitably, the glorious ass.

As a teenager, I noticed asses but was too naïve to know the infinite pleasure they could bring and the power they would come to hold. It wasn't until my mid-twenties that I came to grasp that power. The first butt that sat on my face almost brought an instantaneous eruption from my dick. I was unprepared for the feeling that a big, firm, masculine ass smothering my face would elicit. My next encounter with ass-eating came from a small, tight butt, yet I experienced the same thrill and excitement.

At that point, I began to ponder the infinite variety of asses that existed. We all have our favorites and given my preference for manly, muscular body types, I began to revel in the large, round, firm butt that, for me, has come to define the term "great ass!" It's the kind of butt that is an added incentive for sports fans to watch sports and the kind that makes those uninterested in sports watch anyway. Love of many muscle butt accounts for the large gay viewership of the WWF or any televised event where big, burly, masculine men strut around in skintight uniforms. Seeing butts through tight sports attire is almost as exciting as seeing them nude.

While I've long been a sports fan, it was my growing affection for ass that provided a new dimension to watching athletics, especially football and baseball. If the game ever gets boring, there's always plenty of butt to check out. I only wish basketball would go back to the tight, *short* shorts of the '70s, especially since the players are bigger and stronger than they used to be.

My beloved New York Mets and New York Giants offer up plenty of players with ass-tounding ass-ets: Mike Piazza, Jason Sehorn and Greg Comella, to name a few. When wide receiver Chris Calloway was traded from the Giants a number of seasons back, I missed his consistent play, but mostly I missed his spectacular ass. I even find myself checking in on games that I wouldn't normally watch just to catch some spectacular butt—Shane Spencer of the Yankees or Shannon Sharpe of the Baltimore Ravens, for example. In the world of track and field, not only is Maurice Greene the world's fastest man, he also possesses an ass equally worthy of a gold medal.

So again, what is it about butt? For all my love of various bodies and body parts, a great ass has the best chance of taking my breath away. When viewed from the side or straight on, a great ass holds up. Some butts only look great from one particular angle, but a great ass looks good anyway, at anytime. Of course, it matters to whom that butt is attached, but ultimately you can almost forget what a guy looks like when he has a terrific backside. Ed McCaffrey, wide receiver for the Denver Broncos, is a cute guy in a goofy, jug-eared way, but one look at his meaty ass and he becomes the best-looking guy in the world. His "wide receiver" is almost poetic in its shape and size, featuring awe-inspiring indentations.

For many men—especially rugged, macho types—the ass is a place of vulnerability, the place that could lead to the usurping of their masculinity. But for men able to move past such insecurities, a myriad of pleasures await. Part of my delight in masculine men's asses is the idea that these big, strong, tough guys reveal their vulnerability when presenting their asses to you. It's a covenant of sorts, especially if they don't get fucked. They're trusting you with their cherries, to gain the many pleasures that can occur with the ass—without penetration by a penis.

In a purely visceral way, that is the thrill of the men of Colt, the studio that photographs and glorifies hyper-masculine bodybuilders whose asses are so lovingly and beautifully displayed in all their glory, no matter their sexual predilections. As the safe object of the voyeur's gaze, they are able to pose in ways they probably never would otherwise. Many, I'm sure, get off on knowing men voraciously fantasize about them, though they might be loathe to admit it. Whatever their sexuality, these men present the ideal ass to me, and fortunately they—or reasonable facsimiles—exist in real life, without the filter of the photographer's lens.

When these real-life Colt types pull down their pants for me, revealing their big, round globes, I begin salivating. Initially, there is the visual thrill. Great asses are a pleasure to capture in your gape as they proudly protrude up and out from the body. They demand respect and attention, rising from a pair of sturdy thighs, seemingly defying gravity. Better still is the man with an awesome butt who knows that he's got something special and relishes showing it off in a jockstrap, Lycra shorts or other titillating attire. To see those big meaty melons bursting from the material or framed in white cotton straps from a jockstrap is just one of the many gasp-inducing moments a great butt can provide. I could look for hours on end, but there's work to be done.

Next comes the touch. Feeling a man's mounds brings you one step closer to the ultimate thrill. To feel their strength, their power, their shape can be a religious experience. I love running my hands up those sturdy oaks known as thighs and feeling the exact spot where the butt begins. I love feeling the fullness of the round curves and tracing upward to where the butt meets the back. Taking it all in ... slowly ... with reverence. (Of course, sucking dick while holding onto a butt for dear life is one of life's great pleasures.)

If all goes according to plan, I can position that butt in ways that bring me closer to my nirvana. One position that always make me drip is when a man lies facedown, his legs spread, his ass rising skyward for maximum effect. In this position, you're able to imagine the mysteries that hide within. This is where the vulnerability factor takes hold. The guy is in a passive, trusting position, spread so sweetly, offering himself and his hole, to you.

Feeling the cheeks in this position, with my eyes carefully locked on the hole, gives me an adrenaline rush like no other. I love spending time feeling those cheeks and watching the anus respond to my massaging touch. My thumbs rub close to the pucker, eliciting the first moans and gasps. I love gently rubbing my fingers in the crack and around the hole, getting to know its personality and what it responds to. This position is also great for the butt-munching that will inevitably follow, but more about that later.

My other favorite position is the squat, which was the method employed in my first two encounters. This position provides a startling view of the butt, especially the hole, and offers the more dominant or insecure man a means of controlling the situation and feeling less vulnerable. It also offers a unique perspective from which to experience the full power of a butt: spreading gracefully, visually expanding, consuming your entire line of sight while lowering itself onto your face. It was that power that engulfed me in those early experiences. To have a beautifully-butted man sit on your face is to be in heaven. To feel the mounds envelop your face. To smell his manly musk. To be granted access to that hole that demands service.

Squatting also provides an excellent opportunity for one of

my favorite activities: eating butt. While some prefer fucking, fingering, dildoing or fisting, for true butt lovers, everything begins with a good munch. And this too is where the vulnerability factor comes into play. A masculine man giving up his hole and giving in to the intensity of forbidden pleasure is one of the sexiest things in the world. To feel, see and hear a big, strong guy react to this pleasure can make me cum without touching my dick. The combination of reactions is a buffet of stimulation.

Part of the joy is the mystery inherent in each guy's butt. Each one has distinct zones that elicit the most pleasure. Discovering those zones on each guy is part of the great journey of butt worshiping. Once established, the boundaries can be pushed to achieve the maximum bliss. Eating virgin butt is even better as you experience his initial encounter with the delights we veterans know all too well. It's a remarkable phenomena to see a man let go of his fears and anxieties as he gives way to the actualization of the fantasies that have roamed around his head for so long.

Munching butt is the denouement of butt worship. After all the touching, feeling, admiring and posing is done, it's the ultimate destination. Unfortunately, a great butt doesn't mean a great hole, but when the two come together, it's magic. For me, a great hole is one with a pronounced pucker with just enough give to create the rosebud effect, which makes the munching that much more enjoyable. Smoother holes provide the best work surface—no need to consistently pull hair out of your teeth— though hairy holes have their charms as well.

As with other aspects of butt worship, I start out slowly, gently tonguing the hole and flicking along the pucker. Eventually the full repertoire is brought to bear: sucking the hole, the lips, darting inside, retreating back out again, rubbing my face back and forth, allowing my goatee to provide desirable friction. Again, much depends on the individual's preferences and reactions, but finding out what makes a hole tick is half the fun. Once you've zeroed in on the hot spots, you can raise the bar of the experience and provide hours of stimulation. I love bringing a guy to the brink, only to pull back and then start again. The hole opens up to deeper penetration and the reaction heightens.

The sight of a hot, open, well-eaten hole is breathtaking, making me want to dive back in for more. I love it when a guy shows off his eaten hole, pushing it out, embracing the vulnerability he has displayed and for which has been generously rewarded. Occasionally, I'll pull back and take in the whole ass again, returning to the initial awe, before getting back to work on the luscious hole.

So many glorious aspects to our friend the butt, so much to admire.

After all is said, and mostly, done, there is a sense of accomplishment and intense satisfaction. With the taste of his butt still on my tongue and the sensation of his ass still on my face, I'm able to revel in the experience while it's still fresh in my mind. With my hand on his cheeks, I answer my own query, "what is it about the butt?"

It is mystery and majesty combined. It is that multi-dimensional part of the body that elicits fear and desire in equal parts. For those of us lucky enough to have been blessed with intense admiration of ass, it is a secret we share with other admirers, the fraternity of ass lovers. It is the source of unending pleasure and excitement. It is the holy grail.

Miss Eastview High

RL BALDWIN

The Miss Eastview High School Pageant. If Ms. Davis hadn't asked me to be one of the escorts for the girls, none of this shit would have ever happened. I ain't mad at my parents, though. They did what they thought they had to do. But what do they really think they're solving by sending me to some damn military academy, paying all that money for me to be up here in the damn mountains of North Carolina when all my friends are chilling at Eastview? You know what I'm saying? I'm still the same nigga, still gonna be doing the same shit when I get out of here. Hell, might even start doing it up here. What they gonna do then? Send me to a monastery? I'll be 18 in another year. I'll be alright, regardless.

Damn. The Miss Eastview High Pageant. How should I begin? From the beginning makes sense, huh?

Like I already told you, Ms. Davis—she teaches cooking

and shit like that—asked some of the junior and senior guys to
be escorts at the annual pageant. This meant chilling with all the
fine honeys for practice sessions everyday after school, so we all
were hype about doing it. One day at rehearsal, Ms. Davis had all
the dudes on one side of the stage and all the ladies on the other.
The space backstage was very tight and we were all standing single file waiting for our cues. And you know high school guys. A
lot of them were slap boxing, rapping, wrestling, just being, you
know, guys.

Anyway, I was standing in front of this guy named Vic. Vic
was on the basketball team and we had had a couple of classes
together over the years. We didn't hang out after school or anything, but we were cool. Vic was known to be a ladies' man. He
had a different girlfriend every other week and two girls on the
side in the meantime. Everybody knew Vic was a freak. Actually
the way he used to look at me sometimes kinda freaked me out.
The boy definitely had his own shit going on.

So this one day, Ms. Davis was on stage trying to teach them
ghetto-ass girls how to walk all prissy and dainty and I was just
standing backstage, bored and minding my own business. All of
a sudden I felt somebody touch my ass. I automatically assumed
somebody brushed up against me 'cause the space was so tight,
but then I felt it again. This time a finger pressed against the seat
of my Levi's. That couldn't have been an accident, right? I turned
around. Vic was just standing there looking at me. His right
hand was holding onto the crotch of his pants like boys do when
they talk or laugh or whatever. Ain't that some shit? I looked at
him and he just stared back at me. I hadn't smoked any weed
this particular day, so I know that I wasn't high when I came to

the conclusion: *that nigga just felt on my ass.*

But what was I gonna say? Anyway, what made me the most uneasy was that he thought I might be the kind of person who'd enjoy this. I turned away from him. Then a playful, WWF-like brawl broke out around us and I felt it again.

"You got a fat ass, boy."

"Huh?"

"Fellas, pay attention!" Ms. Davis barked from the stage. "You missed your cue!"

We strutted on stage, grabbed our girls and found our spot in the lineup. I was standing on stage holding hands with Tara Jan, but all I could think about was Vic holding his dick. Did he really say I had a fat ass? Was he really trying to feel on me like I was a girl? And how did this make me feel? Why wasn't I mad?

After two more hours of rehearsal, Ms. Davis—satisfied that all the coeds knew how to walk on and off the stage without falling into the orchestra pit—let us go. I was in the parking lot, getting ready to jump into the little Nissan my momma and daddy bought me, when I saw Vic running toward me, hollering, "Ken, hook me up with a ride home!" Vic had never asked me for a ride before. What was really going on here?

He jumped in before I had a chance to answer.

"I got some weed," he said when we were both inside the car. "Wanna smoke?"

That was a silly question. I never turned down a blunt. But we couldn't get high at my house. My parents would trip if they knew.

"Where can we go?" I asked, pulling out of the school lot.

"My crib. My mom don't get home 'til 'bout 12."

To Vic's we went. Come on now. What's wrong? I'm just trying to tell you what happened that day. What are you tripping on? Everybody at my high school smokes weed. And if you ask me, some of my teachers do, too, but you didn't ask me so I'm not telling.

Anyway, we got to Vic's apartment, closed the door to his bedroom and got smoked out. We made small talk about school, but I wanted to ask him about what happened earlier backstage. But how do you just casually work that into a conversation? Turns out I didn't have to.

"You got a soft ass, nigga."

I looked around the room just to make sure he was talking to me. I mean I know I wasn't the most street nigga ... but damn.

"Vic, you smoke too much, man!" That was the most original response I could think of and you couldn't have done much better under those circumstances either.

"You ever fucked when you high?" asked Vic.

How could I tell him the only girl I ever had sex with was fat Tasha and I *wished* I was high after she took her clothes off?

"Not really." I sat on the edge of the bed. Vic stood up over me, then leaned over my shoulder and put his hand right down my Levi's. This was freaking me out! Not that he was doing it, but that I was letting him! He found his way inside my boxers and touched my bare ass.

"Damn, nigga. Your ass is so hot."

I used to hear the term "hot ass" all the time in reference to a "loose girl." I never thought for a moment that it meant she had a nice ass. The weed had me fucked up. What was I doing? I was letting this dude, who I didn't even know was like that, put his hand down the back of my pants. And I was liking it. Liking it a lot. All of a sudden, I found myself licking on his throbbing dick through his jeans. I couldn't help it. It was right in my face. It felt so good. So natural. With each lick, the bump inside his jeans grew bigger. I couldn't unbuckle and unzip fast enough. His manhood fell out in front of my face and I couldn't stop licking, kissing and sucking it. I couldn't believe I was doing this! It tasted so good. But Vic wanted more.

He stepped back and stood me up in front of him. He pulled my pants down and I was left in just my boxers. Thank God I put on a pair without any holes that day.

"Vic, I didn't even know you were into shit like this. Don't you kick it with Linda? I never cared for her but—"

"What Linda got to do with you and me?"

Shit, what did *I* have to do with it? How did he know? How did he know I wouldn't wanna kick his ass for doing this to me? I never did no shit like this before. How did he know I wanted to?

"Lay down on your stomach," he said.

Even with all the questions in my mind, I didn't hesitate to do as I was told. I felt something oily and sticky running down my backside. Then, without warning, it happened. Damn! Is this what girls feel when they are having sex? The pain was incredible.

Intense.

Immense.

Immortal!

The pain felt like it was gonna last forever!

I arched my back and tried in vain to crawl from underneath Vic's weight.

"Relax, baby," Vic whispered.

I listened, took another pull from the blunt.

"You so tight. It feels so good."

I don't know if it was the sexy tone he was using or the marijuana or both, but it worked. Each stroke felt better and better until I was absolutely sure there was nothing else on earth that could equal the pure pleasure I was feeling. I liked the way he moaned and called me baby. He was breathing so hard, I thought he was gonna have an asthma attack. Way too quickly, he pulled off and blasted all across my back. It was hot and sticky. And there was a lot of it.

Then he flipped me over, ran some of the lotion all over his hand and wrapped his long fingers around my dick. He kept pulling and massaging. I wanted him to do it forever. Then it was my turn to make a hot mess.

"There you go baby. Get that nut."

I can still hear Vic saying that like it was an hour ago.

We laid there motionless and quiet, too exhausted to talk. But then I needed some answers. "Vic, how did you know I would get down like that?"

He fired up the little piece of the blunt that was left. My first after-sex smoke.

"You just know, man." He threw me the towel he was using. "You just know."

"So when did you start doing all this?"

"Nigga, you ask too many questions. Did you like it?"

"Yeah, I liked it."

"Do you wanna do it again?"

"Hell yeah, I wanna do it again."

And "do it again" we did. Every day after school that we could, we did. In school everything was the same. We were just boys. He still had his girlfriends and I still pretended like I liked his girlfriends. But when the last bell rang, I couldn't wait to get to his place for him to take his rightful place.

Tanya Pope won Miss Eastview, but I got the grand prize. Sometimes I still could feel it after I left Vic's house. I was downright giddy. It's like me and Vic had a little secret society that only we knew the initiation rites for.

Everything was going just right until one day, my mom was cleaning in my room and found a bag of weed my stupid ass left on the dresser. Now, her and pops think I have a drug habit. Weed ain't no drug habit. Shit, a lot more crime would be committed if niggas didn't smoke and chill out. Anyway, that is why they sent me to this damn military school. Five hundred boys who can't see their girlfriends unless it's fall or spring break. Five hundred horny and playful boys and little ol' me …

Vic and me are talking about going to the same college and being roommates. Ain't that some shit? And my parents think I have a damn drug problem. If they only knew.

Eternal Shower

MICHAEL GOODWIN

Football practice was over. It was late afternoon and most of the team, coaches and trainers had already abandoned the practice facility and locker room. But I knew that, as usual, one player was still on the field, running extra sprints in between extra push-ups and sit-ups. He wouldn't realize that it was getting late until he looked up and saw the dark clouds gathering in the sky, making the afternoon look like night. When I heard a steady rain begin to pour, I knew he'd call it quits, not wanting to catch the flu before the biggest game of our lives just four weeks away on New Year's Day.

As I lay naked on the slick tiles of the shower room floor, I pictured this stud with his powerful gait—my teammate—bounding across the field to the locker room. The image was enough to send my already horned-up body into orbit. I had been in the showers gently stroking my cock since the last player had smacked his wet towel against a buddy's backside and left the locker room.

Some of the faucets weren't completely turned off, their dripping creating a syncopated rhythm that made me want to beat my meat forever. I often stayed in the showers after my teammates left, the surroundings and my vivid imagination conjuring up some of the most fascinating masturbation sessions I'd ever experienced.

There was a loud crack of thunder, followed by the door to the locker room creaking open. Footsteps pounded the floor and by their weight, I knew it was the massive body of my hard-working teammate who'd had enough sense to come in out of the rain. I heard him flick on a light, then open his locker. Then came familiar grunts and groans as he struggled out of his uniform. Next—I'd spied on him countless times—I knew he'd use one of his enormous limbs to kick his dirty practice uni onto the smelly heap of clothes in the middle of the room. Then he'd swing a towel over his big hairy shoulder and waddle, ever so slightly bowlegged, toward the shower room, farting along the way.

My libido was on fire. I couldn't stop jacking if I wanted to and besides, I didn't want to. I froze but wasn't scared or nervous. He entered and walked right past me, stopping at the adjacent shower, acting as if he were all alone or too exhausted to care about acknowledging a teammate getting off on the shower floor. He turned up the water and grabbed a bar of soap that instantly got lost in his huge hands. I was practically underneath him. His legs were like mammoth columns holding up the biblical temple he called his body. He turned away from me and farted again. I was awestruck.

My eyes locked on the two huge boulders that were his buttocks. They were covered with wet midnight-blue-black hair which thickened near the crevice of his ass. Unassumingly, he cleansed his body of the dirt and grime of a day's practice, and with every movement, his butt changed and created new, mountainous landscapes. His butt in motion possessed god-like grandeur, the greatest story ever told. Hot gushes of water cascaded from his wide shoulders, rushing down the valley of his back, around the curvature of the glorious Maximus and Minimus, heading straight at my face and open mouth. The rivers were so rapid, I had no time to question.

Still with his back to me, he bent over and began washing the gigantic crack of his ass with gusto and verve. His inner thighs and the back of his calves became gullies for the exodus of flood waters. It was as if there were miles between the fault line of his crack and the actual sweet and mysterious hole, that benevolent doorway to his soul.

When the soap rinsed away, I saw clearly how awesome his entire assland really was and nearly melted into the drain pipes. Then he stepped backward, almost colliding with my torso. Still, he ignored me.

The rain outside was as loud as the shower now. Another clap of thunder blended with this wondrous symphony. I beat my cock with increased intensity, not caring if he cared. He soaped up his dick and balls, the action making a succulent "squish" sound as he did.

His dick turned into a rigid swamp root. The head was as large and plump as a summer peach with a hole in the center. He faced me. His eyes pierced mine. A sensuous sneer washed across his lips. He turned around, back and butt to my face again, and straddled my head. Then he began his descent, aiming for my face. The view from underneath was spiritual … his expanding butt cheeks … the parting crack … the walls of pure butt leading up to … the hole … *right there before me!*

It was sacred and demanded respect. It beckoned my tongue. My mouth watered like never before, sweet child-like saliva. It was the most intimate of moments. He was bestowing upon me the most vulnerable entrance into his being, the doorway to his soul, the tubular towers of his chakras and the main highway of his nervous system. It was access to his brain, his heart, his everything.

To think—to actually comprehend—that, with just the touch of my tongue to that magnificent opening, I could reach and communicate with any part of his being. I could tell it stories, give it emotions and feelings like no other form of communication available to mankind. Down long, skin-walls, my lips walked; through pits of hairs, my eyes talked.

My tongue into his butt hole could break ground to a totally different and truthful way of expression.

How utterly awesome.

The infinite array of possibilities.

The "hole-a-lujah" glory of it all.

I lapped and licked and loved and shoved and sucked and swallowed everything and all I could. My mouth and his hole did a *pas de deux.* He pounded his massive meat, flailing it in the air like a monstrous whip, all the while squatting, moaning, gyrating. His balls banged against my Adam's apple with wild passion, sending messages to my soul. *What on earth did I ever do right?* flashed across my mind. Then, with a grunt from deep in his gut, his cock splashed creamy ropes of cum. And while his explosion went on in all its abandonment, my tongue danced in and out of his butt hole, never missing a beat or a message.

Eventually, he let go of his cock and it hung there, moist, tingling, loose, dripping, proud of itself. His cum covered my neck and pecs, tingling on my skin. One of his knees made a loud creaking noise as he straightened up. He paused briefly but didn't turn back. He turned off the shower, but not all the way, leaving a quiet and steady flow that echoed off the tiled shower walls. He left the shower without uttering a word and I imagined him dressing without drying as he always did. A few minutes later, I heard a light switch flick off and then, the door to the locker room close behind him.

I lay still.

I had not cum, but didn't need to.

I felt like I had.

I had never experienced such total emotion, understanding and beyondness as I had with his ass. I knew I was attracted to butts but had never known the why, the what or the *wow* of it.

Slowly I rose, then left the shower as it was, dressed and left the locker room.

It had stopped raining and things were fresh and new. As I walked past the open gym window, I could hear that shower running. There was something eternal about it.

Getting Behind in Business

TROY STORM

"Man, I don't know if I can do this." Charles turned toward me, contemplating the pair of trousers in his hands. We were in the conference room and he was stark naked, his handsome face creased with concern.

My jaw dropped even farther. His tightly constructed, gym-honed body was classically smooth except for a dark triangle of hair nestled between his pecs. It segued to a pencil-thin trail gliding down his washboard abs and pointing to an explosion of dark curls at his crotch. His thick dick jutted out, all solid and fleshy over twin lemon-sized low-hangers.

Normally, the sight of an impressive set of exposed privates of a man whom I had long admired clothed would have had me instantly on my knees in reverent homage to such fine suckable male meat. But I was frozen on the spot, chin soundlessly flapping. Then I was paralyzed by another amazing sight as he turned around: his ass.

Charles and I were Associate Partners at Brubker, Almagore, Fantah and Merle, a very corporate, very close-to-the-vest firm. Four days a week we dressed in expensive, conservative suits and power ties. I had admired how well Charles filled out his on-sale Hugo Bass, but on Dress Down Fridays, which the big bosses only begrudgingly approved, I was always disappointed that he chose to drape his behind in loose-fit J. Press chinos, the cut of which would never reveal the kind of ass I tended to drool over. So, I imagined he didn't have one. Truth to tell, the delectable rumps of our mail room squad—eager, young bucks in shrink-to-fit jeans—tended to draw my attention away from what I supposed was my fellow cubicle mate's somewhat lacking behind.

I also figured the guy was straight. He sporadically dated the available girls in the office, but never seriously, and word was, his energies were focused on climbing the corporate ladder. But I gave it a shot sometimes on dress down Fridays. I never went as far as painted-on denim, but I did do a pair of tailored khakis that had the mail-room boys sniffing around. Charles's "Nice fit, man," was the only rise I got out of him. Those corporate climbers in the mail-room kept me pretty occupied in my off hours, anyway, so Charles's assets and his lack of appreciation of mine didn't weigh very heavily on my gonads.

Until tonight. It was Friday night and we had been hit with a white-hot report that had to be ready by Monday. We were working late and alone in the conference room. After a few hours of dogged, nose-to-the-grindstone work, we had a handle on things, and with a few more hours work over the weekend, we knew we'd able to pull it off in time. By eight, Charles and I were ready for a break. We called out for pizza and beer.

While we were waiting, with a kind of embarrassed shrug, he said, "I've been thinking I should loosen up a bit more and you look pretty damn sharp. I got some new pants."

He went into the executive washroom and came out wearing a pair of flat-front, pearl-gray gabardines that looked like they had been glued on. He turned around for me, modeling.

"What do you think?"

It was hard to articulate. "Panty line."

He looked down, frowning. "Yeah?" He stripped off the pants, then turned his back to shuck his low-cut, snow-white Jockeys. His glutes flexed, his bowling ball butt shifted. My mouth went dry. Then he turned back around, picked up the pants from the conference table and for a few seconds thought about wearing them without underwear.

"Man, I don't know if I can do this." He glanced toward me and noticed I was staring at his dick and balls.

"Oh, sorry," I said. He turned around.

It took a moment for me to realize the most perfect ass I had ever seen on a man had been sinking into the foam of his ergonomically-correct desk chair not six feet across from me for the better part of a year. I spent a blurry few seconds imagining my face buried in the seat of Charles's chair. But that vision instantly morphed into the reality of what was actually within arm's reach. With his back toward me, Charles continued to mutter about whether he could bring himself to wear the pants *au naturel*, while I gloried in the eyeful he was allowing me.

My cubicle mate's butt was a classic. Round and solid, the glutes were strong and well-shaped. His glowing globes bloomed out of a trim waist and were supported by powerfully muscled thighs. A deep canyon was chiseled between the two hard-muscled hillocks and I could only imagine the delicate and tantalizing treasure that was tucked teasingly away. He must spend hours doing fucking squats, I dizzily thought—then flashed on another quick fantasy: being spread-eagled underneath as his ass, clad only in a sweaty jock strap, descended over my head, the motion spreading his hard balls and revealing a trim, black, hair-encircled, puckered butt hole that moistly opened to accept my expanding mouth.

"You okay?" He caught sight of me over his shoulder and turned to peer at me more closely.

I sat in one of the high-backed leather chairs. His crotch was at face level. "Turn around, face away from me," I said. He looked puzzled but complied. My knees sank into the thickly carpeted floor. I smelled his butt, then grabbed his ass cheeks, parted them, and shoved my face forward, jamming my chin into his crack and shooting my tongue against his puckered button.

"What the holy fuck …!?"

Charles tried to pull away, but I grabbed his hips and held on. As he struggled, my tongue squirmed harder against the tightly fluted bastion. The powerful buttocks hugged my stubbly cheeks. His pungent crack, rank with a day's sweat and an instant hormonal reaction blasted its scent deep into my flaring nostrils, watering my eyes and curling my tongue into a narrow arrowhead that drilled against the circular gate.

"Oh … my … go—" Charles leaned forward and grabbed the arms of one of the other chairs. With a gasp, he lowered his face into the seat, arching his ass high and spreading his cheeks. He moaned; I burrowed deeper. The mail room squad had tight little tushes. My lover's butt was beginning to go soft. But Charles's ass was perfect. I intended to give it what it deserved until he chopped me loose.

Miraculously, Charlie wasn't chopping. He was moaning and gasping, moving hand over hand from the leather chair to the surface of the conference table, his face buried in his arms, squirming and shifting to allow me to work his butt for all I was worth.

I licked up and down the crack, swabbing up the sweat, batting his unbreached butt button with my tongue, tearing at the tiny short hairs surrounding it with my teeth as he squeaked and grunted and cursed. The mounds of his ass flexed and tensed and relaxed and flexed again as he writhed under my drilling.

I trailed my fingers up and down the glutes-protected canyon, following in the saliva trail I had laid down with my lapping tongue. My fingertips zeroed in on his butt hole and Charles's muscular torso went rigid.

"Oh, man ... oh, man ... please ..."

I assumed the next word was going to be "don't" and I had no intention of don't-ing. Not on him. Not now. Besides, he didn't sound like he meant it. But *I* sure as hell meant what I intended to do. Within the next few seconds my finger had jammed deep in his hole. Charles sucked in his breath and hissed, but wriggled his butt so that I knew he wasn't trying to throw me off, just trying to get his crazed brain wrapped around the new sensations coursing through him.

His asshole was tight and hot and the wet muscles inside, confused and frantic, erratically fought and sucked in my finger.

I pulled out, added a second digit and drove back in. Charles gritted his teeth. "Shit, damn ..." He pushed his ass back against my hand working his stretched o-ring farther down my two fingers. I chewed at his ass cheeks, running my pebbled tongue over the smooth, flawless mounds and adding my saliva to the ass juices that my sawing fingers extracted from his tight hole. He moaned as I dug around inside, reaming him wide, jabbing for the fat, sensitive prostate. Soon, with a sigh from Charles's heaving chest, his butt gave in and yawned open, begging for more.

I had already worked a rubber over my boner. I was ready. Shoving my pants and shorts down, I stood up and grabbed his hips. He was splayed over the conference table.

"I got a rubber on and I'm gonna fuck your butt, Charlie. Okay?"

"Uh ... uh ..."

I spread his hole with one hand, stretching the resisting flesh wide, aimed my cock with the other hand, fitting its meaty purple head against the trembling entrance to his shit chute and slammed into him. My pubes smacked against his butt cheeks and my nuts swung forward to knock into his perineum. Every inch of me was sunk in his butt. He sucked me up like an engine cylinder sucks up a ramming piston.

Charles pounded the table. Air whistled back and forth through his clinched teeth. His eyes were clinched shut as his head flopped back and forth. His back was covered in sweat. I slowly drew my tool out, dragging his ravaged rectum with me while he froze and held his breath and plaintively shook his head. As I shoved back in, nuts deep, his breath shot out of him like he was bench-pressing two hundred.

"Fuck it, man," he moaned. "Fuck it. Fuck it, hard."

I took my time, pulling slowly out, feeling the frantic muscles inside clutching and grabbing, then reversing to yield and
swallow as I drove back in. I socketed solidly up inside his butt.
His shit hole clamped down the length of my throbbing bone,
hoping to plant me there, but I ripped out again, drawing the
gripping circles of sinewy muscular tissue with me before repeat-
ing the action over and over with increasing fury. I built up speed.
In and out, faster and faster to the sounds of feral grunting and
the slurp and splat of abused tissues colliding. His colon gave up
fighting and let me have my way with his chute, straining to
stretch wider as I grew thicker and harder with each plunge.

Charles's head lolled on his crossed arms, his jaw sagging
open, a drizzle of saliva coursing down his stubbled chin as his
full, moist mouth spread wide in a silly grin.

"I'm fucking coming," he cried, and his body was racked
with rolling jerks as I continued to blast my rambone in and out
of his gulping butt. I imagined his cream shooting out onto the
carpet, momentarily held by surface tension, thick and clotted,
on the tips of the thick pile before the heavy weight of his milk
slowly broke apart and it sank deep into the wool to dry out and
crust and mark it with its fertile male scent.

I needed to get off. My meat was cooking. His ass was so fucking tight and tender I expected him to beg me to haul. But he not
only took it, he kept shoving his butt back for more. I gave him
every inch, pumped up as thick and rock hard as I could manage.
I drove as deep and viciously as I could. My fucking hips ached; my
nuts were numb. He happily took it. He wiggled his butt and
rammed his ass back to meet my forward thrusts. His butt cheeks

were raw and red from the pounding. I couldn't believe Charlie was getting buggered for the first time. He was having too good a time. He seemed to exude some sort of pheromone that numbed my dick and hoisted me to the top of the mountain without letting me shoot in blessed release. I was trapped at the pinnacle of pure pleasure. I had never fucked such an ass. My mind wanted to keep fucking it forever, but my battered body began to rebel.

"You ready?" he growled.

"God, yes," I gasped, teetering on the brink of agony. His sphincter gripped my dick and stripped it like milking a fucking cow. I shot a load that almost sent me into shock from the amount of fluid that spurted out of my body. Over and over I discharged, packing the condom with writhing whip tails as my exhausted frame blissfully spasmed against his loving ass.

Eventually, I was completely unloaded, groggily realizing that getting there was worth every loving ache in my groin. I slumped against Charles's back, gripping his shoulders to keep from sliding off the sweaty, undulating surface. His chute held my dick so tenaciously that even if I did slide off, my exhausted body would be held up by the sheer grip of his butt.

I licked at his neck and gnawed on his earlobe. He grunted and sighed happily.

"That wasn't a cherry butt I just balled, was it, Charlie?"

He snorted. "Shit, man. I was in the Marines. I've fucking missed this butt-busting bad. I had no idea you were interested in my ass." His voice dropped. "Y'know, the gentlemanly thing is now for me to pay you back." He reached back and patted my butt, then shoved his hand in between our sweat-drenched bodies so he could feel my hard dick still stuck up his ass. "Nice fit."

The Thrill-Seekers Luncheon

TROY YGNACIO SORIANO

Most people have a fear of being alone. It's not by accident that the most thrilling words to hear in the English language are "I'm going to come," and not "I'm going to leave." I had been alone for a long time and had forgotten what it felt like to touch and be touched by another young man. Still, I was good-looking by anyone's standards, and when I heard a love song, I would dance and sing along. I had a lot of hope. Strong hope.

I decided a change was needed in my life—maybe more sex, maybe more philosophy—so I got a job at the local museum. I was a tour guide. It was up to me to take people around and explain all the beauty. My employers gave me a brilliant script to say and a maroon suit I loved. Inexplicably, every morning my excitement was the same as if I was going out to a popular night-club. I was full of optimism.

I've always thought that the man who invented nylon deserved some sort of distinguished recognition, and the first time I saw Matthew was the incontrovertible proof of this. He was not wearing underwear, and with the sunlight streaming through his shorts, I could clearly see the outline of his body, his tumescent dick and balls, the ambitious, full arc of his muscular ass in close-fitting, light blue nylon. It was downright cheery.

Standing prominently, framed by the large bright windows of the museum, with a quizzical intelligent expression, I had the sense that there was more art to him than in the entire cold sterile place where I laboured. Frankly, he made all that art look like nothing special. I think if he had stayed in one spot too long, someone would have built a platform under him, took off all his clothes, raised one of his arms, and smacked a fig leaf on his dick.

Forget the Antiquities, the Contemporaries, and even the Post-Moderns. To look at Matt was to see the passion of human striving embodied. His eyes told the story of art: freedom and glory. I wanted to go over to him and kneel. I wanted to kneel behind him and slowly pull down his shorts and press my face into his warm ass. I wanted to make a religion out of it.

With my face resting softly but intently in the cleft of his sweaty ass, I imagined my muffled announcement to the undoubtedly surprised patrons of the museum, something along the lines of: "Ladies and gentlemen, excuse the inconvenience. In this corner we are in the process of setting up a live installation. Everyone, he and I are going to have sex now. No flash photography please. You are about to see fucking art."

It should be someone's full-time job to walk around hold-ing an ornate gold frame up against his ass. Naturally, I mean to suggest myself for this position. Matthew is so fucking beautiful that the first time I saw him, I can honestly say I became teary-eyed and erect at the same time.

He noticed me looking at him and came toward me. I tried to hide my boner and I made the sign of the cross. Conversation was going to be challenging when all I could think about was how much of my tongue I could get up his hairy butthole. He walked up to me and I inhaled deeply. I nodded and smiled politely. I tried to keep in my mind the image of something very civil: a picnic lunch in the garden of a sunny French chateau.

I surprised myself by speaking first, with no respect to my duty as museum official.

"I'm going to say something, and you're probably going to deck me. I have to say it anyway, though."

I was incredibly nervous.

"Your butt is so sexy. I'm filled with this desire to touch you and lick you and fuck you again and again, and just worship you. I know it's inappropriate, and I do ... apologize."

I had said all that with my eyes closed, kind of ready for him to hit me. Or I figured I'd open my eyes and he'd have stormed off. I looked up. He was still there. So I said a little more, speaking with urgency.

"It's just that, I've been looking at your ass for half an hour, with semen running down my leg. You do something to me. You're the most beautif—"

"When does it begin?" He interrupted with a confident flourish.

I laughed with confusion.

"The tour." he said smiling. "When does it start?"

The scheduled tour that day was Impressionism.

Rebelliously, I walked behind the group, sensually distract-
ed by Matt, discreetly checking him out the whole time, his ass,
his face and especially his eyes. He had the most regal bearing. I
found it difficult to talk about all the soft-focus shapes in pastel
colors while Matt was standing there, so startlingly crisp and
vivid. I threw away the script and started saying whatever I wanted. I was glad when it was over and Matt lingered. We sat on a
cold marble bench. I loved that we were alone, surrounded by
historical portraits of disapproving faces.

For an hour, I heard about his life, his interests. Then he
brought up sex. He mentioned he had never been fucked before,
and since I was so interested in his butt, he might want me to do
it. I felt like I had become President, won an Oscar and hit the
lottery all at the same time. I sat there blinking my eyes.

"You want to get fucked?"

He sighed and smiled and stretched his arms sensually.

"Yeah. Basically. I'd love to."

I swallowed hard and looked at the ground.

"And you want me to do it? You want me to lick your asshole and put my dick in your ass?"

"Yeah," he said full of masculinity and humour. "I mean,
yeah!" He looked at me like his request was perfectly reasonable,
which it truly was. Then he added: "That's what I've been thinking about since you said all that earlier."

I was in an amused panic. Not because I didn't want to. But
because I did. So badly. And if I did, I would be conquered by

him, I would be completely his. Doing things for him, doing him, loving him. And I didn't know if I could risk it, my wild heart.

In every museum, there is a room that goes largely unvisited, and we were in that room. Oil portraits of semi-historical figures aren't very interesting to many people, no matter how well-executed they are. We were on the second floor, in a lovely, bright, light-defused room way in back.

The particular museum I worked in was the smallest one in the city and—having been someone's actual home at one point—was privately owned. It looked like a very small castle. I was one of only four tour guides, and it was part of the job that we all had to do double duty as security guards there.

It was a job that you'd only find in Boston, which has its share of eccentric, yet somehow oddly prestigious, well-paid jobs. All day, two employees would do tours while the other two of us would secure the property, and then we'd trade off. Our equipment was low-tech—no stun-guns, just walkie-talkies and police on the speed dial. For the last hour of the day, it was only me on floor two and another guy downstairs. When Matt and I had not seen a single patron after an hour of talking, I turned my walkie-talkie off and took what I considered a not-unreasonable risk in honor of love.

Unzipping my fly, and hoping that no one would be interested in a bunch of paintings of stodgy dead guys, I took his hand and put it on my erect dick. He leaned forward and kissed me. And so it was that we kissed for the very first time. *The Tongue Show*, starring Matt and Troy; 45 minutes long; two tickets only; sold out.

The museum was closing, so we both had to leave. Matt asked for my phone number, but we couldn't find any paper. He remembered he had a banana in his backpack, and it was his idea to "write" my phone number on the banana with his thumbnail. I told him my number and worried a little because I didn't see it appear. "It'll be there in a minute, don't worry," he said with a smile. I told him to just remember that it was there and he stood up, displayed the banana as if it were a dick and glanced back at his ass. He laughed and said, "Oh, I won't forget."

It was three days later when he called me, early in the morning. All he asked me was whether or not I was working that day. When I affirmed that I was, he said, "Okay, I'll meet you at work then. I'm going to give *you* a tour."

I laughed at this, but was insane with erotic curiosity. The day went by, and when I no longer heard any voices in the hallways, it dawned on me that I should look around for Matt. I only walked a little bit when I saw a female co-worker. "Long day?" she said. I thought of my eight-hour erection and replied, "You have no idea."

It was sometimes my habit to write essays and stories in the museum after it closed, which she knew. I told her I'd close the place up and she nodded. When I came back, Matt was standing there in the room we had kissed in, the stodgy dead guy room. Their faces didn't look so disapproving today. Matthew asked me how I was and he touched my forearm tenderly. Then all of sudden, he had an agenda.

"Ready?"

He took me around the museum and showed me all the erotic renderings of the male ass the museum had to offer. I saw a man riding naked on horseback in oils, his lean muscular body shining with sweat. I saw seven playful classical Greek vases; I saw a sculpture of male nude figures engaged in Olympic wrestling. "Notice," he said with a snobbish affect, "how they put a leaf in front of the figure, but leave the back exposed." I saw a pencil drawing of a young man asleep face down in the grass. A poetic depiction of college-aged guys outside in the moonlight: *Nightfootball.*

I had seen all of these works before, of course, but never as a unified collection. The combination of him saying words like "butt" over and over, calling my attention again and again to the curve of a man's ass while gesturing with his hands, made me feel like finding a phone and dialing 911 for lust-induced paralysis. He had to show mercy.

We were back in the room we had first kissed in. He directed me toward the marble bench and I dutifully sat down. He took off his shirt, unbuckled his belt, slid off his jeans, dropped his underwear, hesitated a moment for effect, then turned around. My heart was beating very fast, but I was smiling and happy. He had made a point and it was breathtakingly effective: out of all the art he had shown me, nothing remotely compared to him.

His broad shoulders narrowed down to his trim waist, and right after the place where his belt would be, his skin tone lightened and his ass cheeks came up and out both on the sides and behind him. He had downy, colorless hair all over his butt and dark brown hair around his butthole. His ass struck me as being so masculine, majestic and mysteriously appealing all at once. I wanted to keep a picture of it in my wallet right next to a photo of his face.

He came over and kissed me forcefully, me sitting, him standing. I ran my fingers on both sides of him from his armpits to his waist. I kissed his stomach respectfully and I sucked on his dick. I put my hand under his balls and massaged them and I also massaged his asshole. I got down on the floor and deliriously kissed his feet and sucked on his toes. He was laughing, I was laughing. The fucking stodgy old men were laughing. We were having a great time.

Naked, he ran fast down the hallways of the empty museum, and I chased him. "I'm looking for a room that is more appropriate for me to lose my anal virginity!" he said. It made me laugh so hard that I had to stop. Then I lost him. I walked around calling out to him, but he had disappeared.

I wound up in a large room dominated by Buddhist statues. I said his name and he walked in. He came over and picked up my right arm and brought my fingers to his mouth. He sucked on them for a minute, then brought these same fingers around and behind himself. He moved them between his butt cheeks right to his asshole. Then he guided my fingers to my face and made me smell them. They smelled clean and sweaty. It was his smell and it was deeply comforting. I found it difficult to remain standing, I was so thunderstruck.

There, on the velvet cushioned bench in the middle of the room, I rimmed him thoroughly with his upper body hugging the bench and his ass in the air. I kneaded his butt cheeks with my hands and took my time. I flicked the very tip of my tongue up and down his ass crack and then randomly anywhere on his butt. I looked at his butthole for a long time. Then I grabbed his dick with my hand and put my tongue into his asshole. I was seriously enjoying myself and so was he. He turned around and I looked into his eyes to see how he was doing, and seeing it was what he wanted, I put my dick where my tongue had been.

Yes, I fucked him. Yes, he moaned and squirmed with pleasure. With him beneath me, it appeared as if I were the one "in control." In a sidewalk poll, I would be accorded the title of Top. Only hear me well when I say it would be a delusion not of the *lite* sort to claim that I was the aggressor. I cannot fool myself. That he wanted me to fuck his ass made me giddy with good fortune. It made me smile and be cordial to strangers. It made me daydream and give coin-change to beggars. I would be a fool to think I wasn't a happy slave to his beautiful butt. And so I submitted to him and called myself the aggressor.

But I know the truth.

I feel I have a crush, but crush doesn't fit. Has he crushed me or crunched me? I lay on the banquette, feeling expansive and peaceful. He makes jokes and looks around. I grab my backpack and take my journal out. "Write about my butt," he says, as if commissioning a portrait in a gold frame. Even as he said the words, I knew I would. Because he wanted me to. It was a royal decree and he is my urban prince. I submit I am in love and the world needs to know. I submit, period. We raid the museum kitchen. I put on a CD and James Brown wails throughout the museum. My urban prince is eating and dancing around in his jockey shorts, singing along with James. It is exactly as though he is Prince Valiant and I am little Lord Fauntleroy!

Thanks, Bob

DIRTY TRUCKER RANDY

I'm a truck driver now, but as a recent truck school graduate a few years ago, I found it very difficult to find a job. As a last resort, I accepted a gig with a company that put you in a truck with a more seasoned driver for a few months, then let you have your own truck if you proved capable. I was apprehensive about going on the road with a complete stranger, but I needed a job.

I must have started out with an attitude because my lead driver and I did not hit it off at all. Everything I did was wrong and everything he said pissed me off. When you live with someone in an eight-by-eight-foot square box, it doesn't take long for tension to build. After about six days, I was ready to go home, and he wasn't speaking to me.

One night, on I-40 in Arizona at the top of a mountain pass where they have pullouts for trucks, Bob pulled the rig over and said he wanted to show me how to check the rear differential oil.

I got out in a huff and followed him around to the mountain side of the truck. He had stopped to open the side box, but I did not pay enough attention to notice what he retrieved out of there. With his flashlight, he motioned to a place just on the inside of the fuel tanks where he wanted me to look. I bent over the tank.

"No, down on the inside," he said. I went farther in.

He quickly snapped a handcuff on my wrist. I was so shocked, I didn't fight back. Just as quickly, he brought my other hand up, slipped the cuffs around a cross member on the frame, and snapped them shut. In three seconds, he had me completely helpless, stretched over the fuel tanks.

My first reaction was to get mad. I cussed and called him and his entire family names and threatened him with all kinds of bodily harm. Nothing I said had any effect though and I began to get worried as I kept straining around trying to see what he was doing. But it was dark and I had no idea, until his belt made contact with my pants, my butt to be specific. The belt was leather, about two inches wide, and he began swatting my cheeks with a steady rhythm. It didn't take too many swats for me to realize that he meant business. Since threats were doing no good, I decided to take it like a man and not let him see me suffer. *Thwack … thwack … thwack.* The rhythm never changed, the blows never stopped. *Thwack … thwack … thwack.* I kept thinking that he would tire of his little game, and then I could have my revenge. *Thwack … thwack … thwack.*

Suddenly, he stopped. With no comment, he reached around my waist and undid my pants. He dropped them and my underwear down to my ankles in one quick move. The blows began again. This time … *Zowie!* The pain was incredible. In just a few seconds, I was pleading and making all kinds of promises. Anything to make him stop. *Thwack … thwack … thwack.* Nothing I said brought a response and in no time at all, I was reduced to a blithering sobbing fool. I was crying in that gasping, sobbing way I hadn't done since childhood.

Then the blows stopped.

I slumped onto the tank like a limp rag, still sobbing like a fool. I was grateful that the blows had stopped, but Bob was not through with me yet. He went back to the side box and brought back the squeeze bottle of hub oil we used for the trailer. He squirted a stream of oil on my crack and I began to realize what he had in mind. I had never had a cock up my ass. The only time I'd ever fooled around with guys was with my buddies in high school. "I don't remember anything. I was so drunk," we would say.

"You have been needing a good swattin' ever since you got on my truck, asshole," Bob said from behind. "And I've been needing this for months."

With that, he stuck his cock in my butt all the way to the hilt. The pain knocked the breath out of me. He stood completely still with his dick up inside me and I could feel his crotch hair against my butt.

"Please take it out. Please, please! Take it out! Take it out!"

I felt like I had been impaled on a telephone pole. He stood rigid behind me for several seconds, then slowly backed out 'til I felt his cockhead slip out of me. I was so relieved, I almost started to cry again.

"I'm sorry about the way I've acted," I said with all sincerity. "Please let me loose and we can forget about all of this."

"Just relax this time." He put his hand on my neck and massaged my knotted muscles with his thumb. His cockhead nuzzled up to my asshole and immediately I tensed up. "Relax," he said. "You'll enjoy it more."

Slowly, Bob inched his cock into my asshole. Although it still hurt, the pain was much less. He started a slow in-and-out motion with his cock while his thumb kneaded circles in my neck. Gradually, the pain disappeared and I found myself straining backwards to meet his thrusts. I couldn't believe it, but I was chained to a truck, getting raped and actually enjoying it. My mind was a swirl of confusing emotions. I was completely humiliated and ashamed of my feelings, but I also felt like I was discovering something I didn't know about myself. Could it be that dick was what I really wanted and the lack of it was why I was unhappy with my life?

Bob became completely still. I was amazed when I realized that I could feel his cum spurting through my sphincter muscles, which gripped the base of his cock. I could tell when he finished, and as we both relaxed, I expected him to pull out. But that's not what happened. His cock was not as hard as it had been, but remained deep inside me and Bob made no move to back out. After about a minute, I got restless and wiggled around, thinking he would let me go now.

"Whoa!" He quickly tightened his grip on my neck. "Hold 'er there, we're not through yet."

As if he hadn't humiliated me enough, I began to feel a fullness in my gut and realized that Bob was relieving himself inside me. I was quickly filling up and in just a few seconds, felt like I was going to explode. At this point, I decided that I had had enough. I twisted and turned and succeeded in getting Bob's dick out of my ass. His stream of piss splashed all over my ass, legs and jeans, which were still around my ankles.

"Shit," I said between clenched teeth, "you are such an asshole."

Bob gave a little laugh. "No, son, you're the asshole, I'm a dick. And you can't tell me you didn't enjoy getting your little pussy fucked."

He reached around me and unlocked the cuffs, then rubbed my wrists tenderly to get rid of the numbness. I wanted to hide my shame and pull up my britches—just get the hell out of there and forget this ever happened. What I was going to do about Bob, I had no idea. If I could just get to a phone and off of his truck, I would sort out my confused feelings later. Turn him in for rape? Hell no! I could never bear the shame of what he had done to me if made public.

As I bent over to grab my jeans, Bob grabbed my arms and stopped me.

"I wouldn't get in a rush if I was you, Hoss." He pushed me backward into a kind of squat against the tires. "Give it a minute, you'll see what I mean."

Sure enough, the pressure in my ass built up to a point that I couldn't control my bowels. As Bob walked back over to the side-box, his piss began to squirt out of my ass. When he sauntered back over, he was carrying a flashlight, which he shone on me as I squatted by the truck pissing like a woman. As soon as it stopped, I quickly stood up.

"Not so quick." He settled down on his haunches in front of

me. "You're not done yet." Still shining the flashlight on me, he waited until I squatted again and the pee flowed once more. When it stopped, he clicked off the flashlight and climbed back into the cab. Alone in the dark, I pulled up my soaked underwear and jeans. Not wanting to face Bob, but not knowing quite what else to do, I walked around to the passenger door of the truck and climbed in.

Don't say a word, I prayed. Just start the truck and get me out of here.

I could feel his eyes on me, but no way was I going to look at him. After a couple of minutes of silence, Bob slowly moved into the sleeper. With a gentle but firm hand on my arm, he pulled me in behind him. I still didn't look at him. Tenderly, he took off my soiled jeans. The fight was completely out of me. I just stood there as he stripped me down. He turned me around, then turned on the overhead light. I felt his fingertips tracing the welts he had raised with his belt. Then I felt him cleaning my butt with the Baby Wipes we keep on board for washing our hands. The cloth was cool and goose bumps arose on my ass. Then Bob spread my cheeks with one hand and cleaned my crack of the hub oil he had used to fuck me with.

Somehow, standing there naked, I began to get aroused. I had never had a man touch me in such a personal way, much less stare at my bare butt with the light on. I was past being embarrassed, so I didn't even try to hide my erection as he swung me around. Apparently, this was exactly what he was expecting, because he gently laid me on the bunk and snapped the sleeper lamp out. Quite unlike the rapist who attacked me on the side of the highway, Bob's hands moved lovingly over my body. When he brushed over my cock, an electric current like I had never known shot up my spine.

Cupping my nuts in one hand, he bent over and sucked on my nipple. Moving very slowly with his tongue, he inched his way down my belly to my navel. I knew where he was headed and the head of my dick arched up toward him. Nothing I had felt before that day prepared me for the feeling of my cock sinking into the velvety smoothness of Bob's mouth. In that instant, my life changed forever.

Although Bob proceeded slowly, I popped like a bottle rocket within seconds. He held me in his mouth until I was completely limp, then he covered me up. My eyes were closed from the sensory overload, so he probably thought I was asleep as he moved to the driver's seat, started his Pete, and headed to LA.

I didn't get off of Bob's truck for two more months, although it was a month longer than I needed to qualify for my own truck. Bob taught me many things about life and love as well as about truck driving. I will always remember him and that night.

Thanks, Bob.

Once You've Had Black Ass...

RICK ALEXANDER

While working as a sports reporter for a Big 10 college newspaper, I was blessed with plenty of opportunity to feast my eyes upon some classic jock asses. I've seen dozens of famous butts (and cocks), many of which are now making headlines in the pros. Trust me, my job scribbling down trite sports clichés uttered by cocky young athletes was *not* my prime reason for visiting locker room after locker room for hundreds of postgame interviews. It was the sight and smell of ass that penetrated this reporter's sometimes overwhelmed senses and served as my prime motivation for covering the games men play. If I ever wanna know how many nights I jacked myself raw in college, all I have to do is go back and find out how many basketball, football and baseball games I covered during my four years in school.

And still, nothing prepared me for what I saw one cold evening in Michigan.

It was a snowy February in Ann Arbor, and the hoop world was a week away from its annual bout of March Madness. Several teams in the conference were still jockeying for top seeds and the right to play Eastern Podunk State in the first round of the tournament. Michigan was one of them. That night they beat up on a Big 10 bottom feeder. After the game, I entered the locker room—as usual seeking an interview with an athlete that hadn't showered but was naked, sweat-drenched and ready for a little Q&A.

First off I interviewed a white kid who was always eager to put in his two cents about the game as he saw it from the bench, which is where he'd spent the entire season. I liked the guy though. He had an unfashionable bowl haircut and a Howdy Doody face, but he also sported a freckled-covered ass that was as plump as a basketball. He was shy though and never peeled off his dirty gray jockstrap until the very last minute before heading to the shower.

I was sitting in a chair next to his locker, interrogating his ass—er, I mean, *him*— when I turned my head and found myself eye-level with a huge athletic backside. It belonged to Chris Webber, one of the Fab Five, the group of high school stars who had all chosen to go to UM and win a bunch of titles for the Wolverines. Just as I noticed Webber, he turned away from me and removed the baggy white shorts from his big black behind. I had never been into black men, but that changed (and how!) when Chris Webber's dark chocolate, sweaty bubble butt was inches from my face. His wore a stark white jock and his hairy crack was staring at me. My tongue ached to dive into that black unknown. I broke a personal record for *time it takes to get a hard-on.*

I thanked Howdy Doody and left in haste, fearing one of my fellow reporters would see my tented Dockers and bust me, leading to my permanent banishment from this field of dreams. Chris and his Fab Five went on to a maddening March, coming close to but not winning an NCAA title (ever!), and before I knew it, he'd left school early for the glory and money (and groupies) of the NBA.

But I still have my Chris Webber dreams …

It's the playoffs and C-Webb has just hit the winning shot for the Sacramento Kings. Over the Lakers, no less. The series is over. Kings win. The celebration hits a fever pitch as the team enters the locker room, high-fiving, hooting and hollering and pouring champagne over each other's heads. I observe like a wallflower for a minute, then move into the chaos, inhaling the musty smell of the locker room. Ah, the aroma of ass and testosterone! I'm the C-Webb of sports reporters, so I get to interview the game's hero before anyone else.

"Anything for you," Webber says with a smile and a wink. "I already know what you wanna ask me."

Unfazed and professional, I ask about the winning bucket, defensive strategy against Shaq and Kobe, the significance of the win for the city of Sacramento. He answers all my questions, and as he does, he undresses, never taking his eyes off me.

You will be okay, I say to myself. Concentrate.

Normally, the noise around us would be deafening, but I can hear every word he says as clearly as if we're the only two people in the room. "How does it feel finally getting over the hump and beating LA in the playoffs?" I ask. C-Webb laughs and turns away. He props his leg up on a bench and removes his shorts, leaving on his soaking wet jock. Outta nowhere, he grabs both his butt cheeks and spreads them open. I'm in shock, I have to sit on the bench. He sees this and bends forward, coming even closer to my face. For the second time in my life, I'm inches away from Chris Webber's dark chocolate, sweaty bubble butt. He looks at me as if he has full awareness of this historical factoid and says:

"Go ahead, taste a winner."

I want to run, but I'm not stupid. I want to look around to see if any other ball players, reporters, cameramen, trainers, team owners or ball boys are looking, but I can't. Every single decibel of noise evaporates. A cone of dusty light descends from above and envelopes us. Beyond us, the celebration continues in slow motion. Nothing else matters. No one else exists in our little world inside the cone of dusty light. The sweet sweaty smell of Chris Webber's asshole invades my nostrils like a trail of smoke and stops me in my tracks. As if that were his very intention.

He backs his hairy ass up to my face.

"Eat my fuckin' ass, man! You won't get a third chance to blow it."

I've heard the magic words. I waste no time. My tongue slithers in faster than a school of minnows trying to escape a starving salmon. He moans and impales his ass on my tongue.

"Eat!" He pushes his cheeks together and squishes my face, then spreads those same cheeks apart and lets me in. He alternates the squishing and spreading movement and I feast. My tongue starts to cramp, but he grabs the back of my head and forces it deeper into his ass. I taste funk. I taste curly black hairs. I taste the game-winning shot.

He squirms and releases his huge NBA cock from his jock-strap. With the same hand that brought down Shaq and Kobe and the city of LA, he jacks off until he releases a load that shoots skyward like the champagne elsewhere in the locker room. I rim his ass until his cum has finished coating the ceiling. Then he turns and rams his manhood down my throat. I clean off the layers of cheesy sweat that come from two and a half hours of hardcore balling on national TV.

Too soon, Chris is satisfied that I'm done. He grabs a big white towel. The cone of light fades. The volume of the celebration increases and our immediate space gradually merges with the world beyond.

"Thanks," he says in his deep husky voice. Then he disappears through the crowd and heads toward the showers.

Azzpork, the Horny Ghost

GREYSON B. MOORE

Joaquin was thoroughly tired and perfectly pleased with his new apartment. He surveyed the front room, seized a wooden crate and sat down. He looked around and tried for the umpteenth time to figure out how he got such a nice apartment for such low rent. As he sat pondering, he heard a knock at the door. He opened it.

"I heard someone rented the place again," said the old woman who stood in his doorway. "I wanted to see who the fool was."

"Fool?" Joaquin repeated. "Thanks for the wonderful welcome."

"You'll be out in six months like all the others." The old woman cackled. "Place is haunted." She swung around, entered the apartment across the hall and closed the door.

"Old witch." Joaquin slammed the door shut.

He was hot and sweaty from moving, so he headed for the bathroom and a shower. As he undressed, he thought he saw someone in the mirror. It was a good-looking black man with processed hair and a pencil-thin mustache. He was holding a saxophone and reminded Joaquin of Duke Ellington in his younger days. "The ghost must have been a jazz man." Joaquin said jokingly as he rubbed his eyes. "Old hag putting ideas in my head."

The shower was in a tub, so Joaquin had to lift his leg to get in. As he did, it felt as if someone or something pinched his butt cheek.

"Ouch!" He rubbed the spot, then lifted his other leg and felt a similar pinch on that cheek. Had he pulled a muscle during all the moving?

He turned the shower on and could swear it was saying "nice rump, nice rump" as it squirted water out of the showerhead. Joaquin laughed and noticed that his dick was getting hard. "Sick," he said as he lathered himself up. He dropped the soap, bent over and felt a firm slap on his butt. This time he let out a loud yelp and turned around. The warm water splashed against his butt. He looked at his butt cheeks and was startled to see what appeared to be an imprint of a large hand on his golden brown buns.

"Naw. Must be from something I sat on."

He rinsed himself off, wrapped a towel around his waist and headed for the bedroom. He was about to sit down on the bed when the towel fell. He bent over to pick it up and noticed a pair of wing tip shoes a foot away from his face. Cautiously, he looked up. Standing before him was the man he had seen in the mirror.

"What ... who ..." Joaquin stood up and tried to sound brave.

"I need a roll in the hay," said the man. Joaquin had a stunned look on his face. The man laughed. "Or whatever you crazy kids are calling it these days. When you've been dead since the '40s, you kinda lose touch with the current slang."

"You're the ghost." Joaquin tried to keep his voice from quivering.

"Depends." The man winked. "If you've heard I'm in the life and like to cornhole, then, yes. And you sure have a fine rear."

"I don't do that stuff." Joaquin pulled back and puffed out his chest. The ghost snickered. The ghost's clothing vanished and he stood naked and unquestionably erect. He drew closer to Joaquin. "Back in my day, we colored menfolk looked after each other's needs. Especially when the band was on long road trips. So I know the look when a man wants it in him. And you want it. Now stand up and bend over, I want to take a good look."

Before Joaquin could react, his body moved on its own and he found himself bent over, butt facing the ghost.

"Mighty fine, mighty fine." The ghost slapped Joaquin's taut rear. Joaquin looked around and recognized the hand print. "How old are you?" asked the ghost.

Joaquin stood up. "Twenty-eight, why?"

The ghost shook his head. "Young colored man in the prime of your life and never had another colored man play with your butt. *Tsk, tsk.* I feel sorry for you. In my day, your butt would have seen more wieners than Oscar Meyer. Especially with you having such a fine bottom."

Joaquin was flattered by that remark.

"I bet you have never been tongued either."

Before he could reply, the man disappeared and Joaquin felt something warm and soft passing quickly over his anus.

"Feel good?" said the ghost, who was now behind Joaquin.

Joaquin refused to respond. The forces that were controlling his body made him bend over and the soft, wet object pushed harder and harder at his anus, trying to gain entry. Joaquin didn't try to stop it. In fact, he pushed out his butt lips so more of the sensitive tissue would be available to the probing tongue. When the rimming stopped, he stood once again and let out a very audible and disappointed sigh.

"Get on your stomach on the bed," said the ghost, "and put a pillow under your belly."

Joaquin knew what was going to happen next whether he liked it or not, so he decided he might as well not anger the ghost. He lay down, waiting for the moment of penetration. Time passed and he wondered if a ghostly organ could be felt at all. More time passed and curiosity got the better of him. He rolled over and found that there was no one else in the room. Joaquin had never felt so alone.

Days passed, then weeks. Joaquin wondered if he would ever see the ghost again. He wondered if the ghost had gotten what he wanted and had no reason to haunt anymore. He also wondered if the ghost had somehow discovered that his anal cherry had been popped a long time ago, and as a result, no longer trusted him.

He begged the ghost to come back and enter him, but nothing happened. He even displayed his bare butt in various seductive positions around the apartment, but the ghost didn't materialize. He was near madness when he stood on an overstuffed chair and bent over and begged, "Cornhole me now!"

A chill went down Joaquin's spine.

"Just wanted you to beg for it," said the ghostly voice.

Before he could respond, Joaquin was penetrated. He moaned as the ghostly organ slid into his anus.

"That's one smooth ride," said the ghost. "Knew you couldn't be pure."

Joaquin felt his body tremble and his prostate pulse. "I'm having an orgasm in my hole," yelled Joaquin in amazement.

"You need another one then," said the ghost.

"I can't take another one," Joaquin screamed, but the orgasm swept over his body anyway.

"Your butt deserves more," said the ghost, refusing to withdraw.

The chair overturned. Joaquin fell to the floor. The ghost kept fucking him and he experienced another powerful anal orgasm. When it was all over, he felt a firm slap on his rear and heard:

"Next time you want it this bad, just say, 'I want my Azzpork.' And I will come to you."

The ghost dematerialized.

Joaquin was startled by a knock on the door.

"You all right in there?" It was the old woman across the hall. "I told you the ghost would get you. You'll be out of here in six months, just like all the others."

"Doubt it, old lady," he said laughingly. "I seriously doubt it."

Stone Cold Steve Austin's Ass

PETER MORSHEAD

Recently I attended one of the big World Wrestling Federation matches at the local sports arena in my city. While everyone was there for their own personal reasons, mine was one of pure lust. And the object of my lust was wrestler Stone Cold Steve Austin. That night, I was a man on a mission: to boldly go where no gay man had gone before: up close and personal with Stone Cold's naked ass.

No other WWF wrestler possesses his particular brand of cocky, arrogant, in-your-face attitude. I love it, major turn-on for me. Stone Cold is a man's man: 6'3", 255 pounds of solid beef, shaved head, goatee, moustache and piercing blue eyes. A beer-drinking, jeep-driving, foul-mouthed dude who does what he wants when he wants on his terms. It's his way or the highway.

Whether that's just his wrestling character or he's that way in real life, I don't care. I worship him. He is the epitome of the macho persona I love.

Most of all, I love to watch Stone Cold Steve Austin's ass. Oh, man, what an ass. The dictionary definition of "perfect." His ass cheeks are high and tight and big—just the way I like them. Seeing him in a tight T-shirt and faded blue jeans is enough to make my cock instantly jump to attention. I love how jeans form-fit his ass, as if the pants were specially made just for his incredible body. I can only imagine the effort involved in years of doing squats to achieve such a great ass.

After Steve's match that night, he left the main auditorium for his private dressing room. I'd watched the entire thing with an erection and my cock was still rock hard. I tend to leak a lot of precum, so the front of my underwear was soaked. I surveyed the thousands of fans around me, hero-worshippers just like me, knowing I had to brainstorm a way to get backstage to get a glimpse of the mother of all asses.

Before the next match, a fight broke out in the ringside seats. A handful of guys started slugging it out and an entire posse of security guards rushed in to break up the action. It was just like a scene out of an episode of the WWF on television. I watched the madness for a while, then decided to go take a piss before the next match. As I made my way down the stadium steps in search of a restroom, my curiosity about the fight won out over my need to pee. I found myself standing on the arena floor, mesmerized by the testosterone-fueled action. The guards were having a field day trying to break up the guys who were fighting and I suddenly felt myself being nudged forward by a mass of bodies behind me. Then the fans nearest the melee got in on the action, pushing and shoving, yelling and swearing, hurling metal folding chairs.

I decided to get the hell out of there. I didn't come here to end up in the hospital or jail. I came here to get as close as I could to Stone Cold's ass. I turned to leave. My eyes caught sight of a laminated security pass on the concrete floor several feet away. It must have fallen off one of the guards during the scuffle and was getting trampled on, kicked around, abused.

A light went off in my head. I moved toward that pass like it was a thousand dollar bill on the sidewalk. My ticket to paradise. Do not pass go; do not collect $200; go straight to those two fleshy mountains of heavenly muscled butt belonging to your hero. Snagging that pass was more important than oxygen. The prospect had my adrenaline pumping. My heart was racing and my cock was hard as a bullet. I shoved my way through the crowd like a desperate man. Some jerk behind me shoved me hard and I fell flat on the concrete. Good idea, I suddenly realized, reminding myself to thank him later. I scrambled to my knees and crawled between the legs frantically shuffling all around me. I got so close to the pass, I could almost reach out and touch it; but a huge black boot was about to kick it across the floor. I dove like a linebacker scrambling for a fumble.

Bingo! Touchdown! There is a god. Maybe.

After I escaped the donnybrook, I took about a hundred deep breaths and found the tunnel where I'd seen the wrestlers enter and exit. It was a long, factory-like concrete hallway, nothing glamorous, just the underbelly of the gladiator's palace. Once there, I clipped the pass to my jacket and kept walking, trying to calm myself down and make some kind of attempt at looking normal. I walked toward a small, sedate crowd gathered at a roped-off entrance that sure as hell looked like the way to the dressing rooms. I walked calmly past groupies and security guards who gave me and my pass a quick glance, then looked away. Yep, I thought to myself, eyeing all the doors in my periphery, these are the dressing rooms.

There were other anonymous faces I passed, media types, trainers, other jock supporters. I also noticed other wrestlers. They could have all been telephone poles for all I cared. Trying to stay calm, I glanced at the names on some of the dressing room doors. Then, on one of the doors near the end of the hallway, the name that made the butterflies in my stomach shift into overdrive: S. C. STEVE AUSTIN.

No time to think. I went inside and shut the door.

Immediately, I hid behind a bank of lockers, peeked farther into the locker room and saw a very large mirror that reflected images from even deeper inside. The mirror treated me to a sight I would gladly have paid $500 to see: Stone Cold Steve Austin in all his glory! He was wearing his black wrestling trunks, black knee pads and black wrestling boots. He gulped down a can of beer, then tossed the can into a nearby trash can, belching loudly as it landed. My mouth went dry. My hands were shaking.

He turned his back to me, put one foot on a wooden bench and bent over to unlace his boots. This afforded me a great view of those big firm mountains of man butt. I wanted to move closer, run my hands over them, but I also didn't want to startle him and have him freak out over an obsessed fan in his dressing room. I remained in the shadows and enjoyed the view.

After he took off his boots, socks and kneepads, he peeled off his sweaty black trunks and tossed them on the wooden bench. Then he stood in front of a full-length mirror, admiring his sexy, muscled body. This god of masculinity was a site to behold. Since his back was to me, I still had a perfect view of the globes of his ass. I licked my lips, longing to bury my face between those two mounds of butt flesh.

Steve scratched his balls, then walked toward another room that contained the toilet and shower stall. I held my breath as he walked, my eyes drawn down past his powerful arms and pecs to his swinging, flaccid dick meat between his massive thighs. His cock looked to be about six inches long in its soft state and he had a huge set of low-hanging nuts. As he disappeared into the shower, I got a quick look at his ass from the side; it looked even more beautiful in profile, his ass cheek making a perfect curved arc, so firm, so masculine. My cock was so fucking hard, I had to glance down to see if any of my precum had soaked through my jeans. Nope, everything was okay.

I heard the shower running and the sound of a curtain being pulled shut. Quickly, I stole past the entrance to the shower, not daring to turn my head for fear of Steve catching me. Then, right before my eyes on the bench, was the pair of trunks Steve had worn to wrestle. To me, they were the greatest piece of clothing in the entire world at that moment. I had to at least touch them. Or even pick them up and savor the musky scent of ass and crotch sweat. My eyes were glued to the pair of trunks. I was a junkie whose next fix was before him. My heart pounded so fiercely, I thought it would explode in my chest. I picked up the trunks. To think that I was holding Stone Cold

Steve Austin's sweat-soaked wrestling trunks that had covered his big sexy muscle butt was enough to make me want to whip out my cock and fire off a hot load of cum all over the place. I shoved my face into those trunks and took deep whiffs. Oh, fuck! I almost came right then and there. I rubbed the sweaty trunks all over my face and sniffed the areas where his balls had rested and where his ass had been. If they could bottle the great musky man scent of Austin's crotch and ass, I'd buy it by the case.

I should've been blasted out of my reverie by the sound of the shower being shut off and the shower curtain being pulled back. And had I been sniffing anyone else's funky drawers, I probably would have. But this was the man whose posters and photos were plastered over my bedroom walls. I was in another world in his trunks. And I didn't realize that Stone Cold Steve Austin himself had finished showering and had joined that world until I heard:

"Well, well, what do we have here? A fan who likes the smell of my funk." He was rubbing a towel over his pecs and under his pits, his dick swinging in front of him. He was also grinning a lopsided, shit-eating grin, the corner of his lip upturned in a cocky snarl.

My heart stopped; my mouth wouldn't. "I'm really sorry ... I'm a big fan ... I was just trying ... souvenir ... I'll pay for the trunks ... so sorry, please, don't—"

"I could have your man-funk loving ass thrown in the slammer, you know." He stood there, not backing away, not coming closer. "There you'll get all the funky man-funk you want. 'Course, it won't be Stone Cold's sweet ass man-funk, now will it?"

"I'm sorry, sir."

"Why you like my man-funk, boy?"

I babbled, uttered words I was too nervous to hear.

"You like the smell of Stone Cold's crotch and ass, don't you? Gets you off to know what a real man smells like, huh? Nothing gets a man's smell more than his crotch and ass, and that's what you like about this real man, ain't it, boy? Admit it."

As anxious as I was, I noticed that his cock was starting to grow harder, which made me even more tongue-tied.

"I like ... man ... not afraid ... sweat ... work hard."

"Son," he said, interrupting me.

"Yes, sir?"

His towel dropped to the floor. His massive dick fattened and grew longer. "Shut the fuck up and kiss my ass."

"Excuse me? Did you ... are ... sir ..."

"You're babbling again, damn it." He advanced toward me. "Kiss. My. Ass."

"Do you mean it? In a good way or bad way? I mean—"

"Are you gonna kiss my ass or do I have to body-slam you?"

"I wanna, yeah, I mean, if you want ... me ..." My mouth started to water in spite of my nervousness. I'd heard stories about groupies, but I figured they were just females.

"It's your lucky life, boy," Stone Cold said. "You're into the one thing this man never gets enough of: a tongue trying to earn the respect of my sweaty asshole."

Stone Cold faced the wall, bent forward, stuck out his massive butt and spread his muscled legs wide.

"Your face, my ass, now."

I needed no further invitation. I dropped to my knees and

was inches away from masculine, beautiful, manly perfection. I could have stayed there for hours admiring the acres of ass in front of me, but I had my orders. Carefully I put a hand on each butt cheek. They were warm to the touch. I massaged and rubbed his ass and kneaded his butt cheeks like they were bread dough. Thick, thick muscles. Steve emitted a soft deep groan of pleasure, encouraging me. I moved closer and started licking his ass cheeks.

I was a starved man at an all-you-can-eat buffet. I licked and kissed each perfect cheek. There was a light dusting of blond fur all over his ass and in his crack, which only added to my enjoyment. My tongue ran over each melon, from the top where they connected to his back, right down to where they met his legs. A bomb could have detonated next door and I wouldn't have cared. All that mattered was the fact that my face was buried in the ass of my hero, my idol, the biggest, sexiest, bad-ass stud in the WWF, and he was loving it. I was on top of the world.

Stone Cold let out moans and gyrated his ass. I moved his cheeks apart; he spread his legs wider and leaned forward more, thrusting his ass toward me. My tongue met his puckered pink hole and gently lapped around the opening.

"Oh, fuck, yeah! Shit, buddy, that feels fuckin' great. Yeah!"

I was leaking precum and getting off on the sound of Stone Cold's husky voice. I prayed this wasn't a dream I'd be waking up from. I never wanted it to end. I kissed and sucked that asshole more intensely and managed to get more of my tongue up there.

"Hell yeah!" Steve said while grinding his asshole down on my mouth. "Oh, man, that's fuckin' great. Yeah, eat out Stone Cold's ass. Yeah, buddy. Oh, yeah, that's it, buddy. Tongue out

Stone Cold Steve Austin's shitter. Yeah! Aw, shit, that feels so fuckin' good."

The spit and drool dripped off my chin as I slurped and ate out his ass. I worked a finger up his asshole, which was now quite relaxed and wet with my saliva.

"Oh, shit!" he hollered.

I reached around and grabbed Steve's massive cock. It must have been at least nine inches. I cupped and massaged his egg-sized nuts. Then I inserted a second finger up Stone Cold's hole. He let out another groan and pushed his ass farther down on me. I had my fingers up the most powerful butt in wrestling, sensually rubbing the soft insides of his hole while Steve moved his ass up and down and stroked his cock.

I moved my fingers slowly around the insides of Stone Cold's asshole, marveling at how wonderfully tight he was. Oh, man, could it possibly be that he had never taken a finger up his butt hole? The thought that I might be the only male in the entire universe to pop Stone Cold Steve Austin's cherry made me even hornier. I felt like a celebrity myself! This god of masculinity and testosterone was right in front of me and his sweet manly ass was all mine at this very moment. I couldn't take it anymore. I would never get another chance like this. I needed another fix of Austin's ass and *now!* I removed my fingers and dove between those big meaty cheeks, a firm grip on each cheek, spreading them wider, determined to get my face deeper and deeper inside his warm, salty crack.

"Aww, yeah, buddy!" said Stone Cold. "Come on, fucker, that's it! Taste my fuckin' ass, boy ... yeah, boy, eat out that sweaty man ass. You ain't never had it this good, boy."

His husky growl filled the locker room with the words I needed to hear. The man of my dreams was loving every minute of my mouth and tongue. Steve's crack gave off a lot of heat, and the hair along the crack and around the hole captured the warmth along with the musky smell of sweat. The short shower hadn't completely washed away his manly scent. I took deep whiffs of his aroma to lock the memory in my senses forever.

Stone Cold kept pumping his meaty cock and gyrating his ass around as I feasted. I kissed his puckered hole with confidence and pushed my tongue inward with even more force. He let out a deep groan, his massive hand groping for the back of my head. A calloused palm collided with the side of my face and slid over my ear to the back of my head. I was forced downward to the point that all I could feel, taste, smell and breathe was Stone Cold Steve Austin's massive ass crack and that sweet, sweaty hole. I was gasping for air, but I didn't care and neither did he: Stone Cold didn't stop smothering my face with his ass.

"My bitches don't eat me like you do. Oh, fuck, you like that, don't you? Come on, fucker, eat Stone Cold's big ass! Yeah, that's it … oh shit, man. Get your … fuckin' tongue … up my shit hole … you fuckin' ass-eatin' bastard! Eat the best man ass ever, boy! You're eatin' the best and don't fuckin' forget it!"

I squeezed his beautiful mountainous butt cheeks and rubbed my face all over his blond hairy cheeks, trying to imprint my face in them. Strong whiffs of his musky crotch sweat filled my nostrils. Stone Cold's body was on fire. I bit down on his right cheek and he tensed up and growled. His legs were quaking and I knew he was close to shooting. I inserted my fingers back into his hole, now much more loosened, and he groaned and thrust his hips back and forth on my fingers until they were buried past the knuckles.

After a few minutes, he turned around and my fingers came out of his hole. He grabbed me by the back of my hair and shoved his hard prick in my mouth. I tried not to gag as he pounded my throat with his massive Stone Cold cock. He was circumcised and thick, with a thick vein running down one side of his shaft. I could smell a faint musk from the blond fur of his crotch, and it gave me more fuel to keep sucking his big prick. I reached under and pushed two fingers up his hole and he thrust his hips forward, driving his meaty shaft deeper down my throat. Stone Cold pounded away. Before I knew it, my nose was meeting his musky blond pubic hairs. I cupped his massive nuts and massaged them. I could tell from his breathing that he was close to cumming.

"Oh yeah, fucker! That's it ... suck my big fucking prick ... oh, fuck ... yeah, suck it ... eat Stone Cold's cock ... yeah, buddy ... fuck, that feels great."

Stone Cold vise-gripped the back of my head. With a low growl, he pumped thick ropes of hot cum down my throat. I swallowed as best as I could, but a lot of the cum dripped out the sides of my mouth and off my chin. His cum was bitter and tangy. I wanted it bottled and sold.

I still hadn't cum yet, but Stone Cold looked down at me with that cocky sneer on his face and patted my head. Then he went over to where the black trunks were and picked them up.

"I believe you were wanting to take these with you." He wiped his crotch and ass with them, then tossed them at me. I caught the trunks and stuffed them in the inside pocket of my jacket. I wouldn't sell them for a trillion bucks.

"Thanks, Stone Cold!"

"I could still have your ass thrown in jail, you know." It didn't sound like a threat, just a statement. "Now get your ass out of here before I change my mind. And that's the bottom line 'cause Stone Cold said so."

I nodded and smiled and he winked at me. I thought of asking for his autograph, but I figured why bother. The smell of his ass on my face and his cum in my belly were ten-zillion times better and more memorable than any autograph.

And that's the bottom line.

Gay Sushi

JOSE LOUIS MUÑOZ

Famine that would not be satisfying until I gently lay my gay sushi on satin sheets. There, resting comfortably and moving very slowly, sleeps what I am about to eat. The hunger one feels for nice warm gay sushi, what can a man do? I stand right in front and I make my hands do the dirty work. I spread the savvy food open and there, right in the center, the wonderful red sushi. It moves ever so gently, and you can almost hear it whispering, "Eat me," "devour me," "make me loose control."

I, like a faithful customer, obey the pleas, my lips like two out-of-control sex slaves and my tongue a drill. An uncontrollable drill, that will not be stopped until it reaches the deepest zone. I let the fluids in my mouth merge with the copper smell of manhood. I feel no shame, no regrets, just a lusty and dirty feeling that arouses more my own flesh. Oh, my gay sushi, how I'd love to be able to consume it all day. Eat until exhaustion makes me weak at the knees. When you feel the warmth of that special gay sushi, your own man tool becomes a instrument. One, just one, that's all you need to enjoy the gratification of being a member of this special food club. There, between two raw flesh walls, the senses can hold no longer the magnificent pleasure of gay sushi.

I have sinned and my body does not care. I thrust and thrust my desires and my hunger deep and deeper. I feed the famine until he can no longer withstand the river of satisfaction and erupts with the cream of life right on top of the tasty sushi. I am not thankful yet. Like a hungry animal, I once again put my mouth on the gay sushi, now covered with cream, and I eat. How I have driven my tool to erupt again while my body with every motion begs me to stop and I don't. I want more. I want the gay sushi to plead for more. I yearn to hear from its senses, without words, not to stop, to keep feeding me until tiredness takes over.

I can no longer stand, so I just lay my face gently on the gay sushi I have just eaten and rest. Dreaming of the chance to make of it yet another buffet.

Night Patrol

JAMES COPELAND

Matt Hundley stormed into the locker room and flung his hockey stick against the wall of lockers. He had hustled his ass off for six months: training, practicing, racking up 28 goals and 31 assists. He had earned the respect of his teammates, family, minor league scouts and even those who had doubted him. But none of that mattered now. His team had just blown it. A shot at the final round of the collegiate playoffs had slipped through their fingers. The season was over.

He sulked past the other players in their various states of undress, the smell of sweaty men and hockey gear strong in the air. He opened his locker, stripped off his equipment and threw it in his hockey bag, smothering the bottle of champagne that Steve, the team goalie, had purchased for the celebration that was now permanently canceled.

Matt was the first in the showers and began scrubbing the sweat off his sore body. Steve entered with a semi-hard cock and gave him a playful smack on the ass. A good grudge fuck usually calmed Matt when he was pissed off, and Steve, a submissive bottom, knew how to take full advantage of his buddy's angst-fueled lust. Normally after a bad game, the two would retreat to Steve's dorm room and down a few beers. Then Matt would nail the goalie's tight ass a half-dozen times, shooting load after load all over Steve's muscular back. But tonight sex was the last thing on Matt's mind. He ignored his fuck-bud and finished showering, telling himself he'd apologize tomorrow.

It was an unseasonably warm night for late March. Matt tossed his gear into the trunk of his restored '69 Mustang, slipped into the driver's seat and slammed the door. He pounded his fists against the steering wheel and cursed. Then he keyed the Mustang to life, peeled out of the parking lot and headed for the interstate …

State Trooper Alan Faraway's cock was stiff and aching. Like most cops, his hard visage was calm and controlled, but beneath the uniform and badge was a man. And buried within the man were the primal needs that required frequent attention. He glanced at his watch. His tour would not end for another three hours, but the ache in his loins could no longer be denied. It was a slow night on a virtually empty highway, his prowler obscured by a line of low bushes. He unzipped his baggy trooper pants and fished inside his jodhpurs. Like some Navy SEALS and other Marines he knew, he didn't wear underwear, didn't believe in it.

He loosened his gun belt and pulled out his circumcised meat, which stood erect between his splayed legs like a soldier standing at attention. His cock grazed the cool metal of his belt buckle. Shivers slid up his spine. He reached underneath the seat for the stained cum rag and placed it on his stomach. The suspension of his Caprice Classic jounced ever so slightly as he stroked. Moments spun into minutes. The juice inside his balls churned. His muscular thighs opened and closed repeatedly in a steady rhythm. His blue eyes narrowed, his thoughts somewhere in his Marine Corps past and his ten years as a drill sergeant.

Those days, he had no trouble finding young grunts in need of extra discipline. He'd march 'em into the woods, order 'em to strip and drill 'em with grueling calisthenics in the nude. Then he'd gag their mouths, tie 'em to a tree spread-eagled and give them a good ass-paddling. After that, he would unbutton his BDUs, spit on his cock, and slide ten inches of discipline up their tight asses, taking them over and over until he was spent. Some of them stubbornly refused to learn their lesson the first time and came back for more.

The images of those hot days and nights had him on the verge of shooting his load into the cum rag. But suddenly his radar gun shrieked, registering a reading of 75 miles-per-hour in the red LED. Headlights illuminated the cabin of his cruiser. A vintage Mustang roared past. "Shit," he muttered. His concentration was broken, the momentum lost. Angered by the interruption, he started the Caprice's engine, flipped on his headlights, toggled his roller lights and siren and engaged a pursuit with his hard cock still poking out of his pants …

Metallica was blasting on the CD player and Matt didn't notice the red warning glow coming from his muted radar detector until it was too late. "Oh fuck!" he hissed as an array of strobe lights filled his rear view mirror. He wanted to flee but knew it was futile. He steered over to the breakdown lane and the patrol car pulled up right behind him. He shut off the CD and dug his license, registration, insurance and PBA card out of his wallet. He wasn't sure if the PBA card would get him out of a ticket, but it was worth a try.

State Trooper Faraway radioed-in the Mustang's plates while tucking his cock back into his pants. So far the car was clean, but the undiminished ache in his balls had him miffed. He grabbed his Stetson, exited his cruiser and began a slow, arrogant stride, noticing the various hockey stickers on the back window of the Mustang. He shined his flashlight into the car, searching for weapons, drugs or alcohol, but only found the worried expression of the young male driver looking back at him. Faraway took mental note of the boy's green eyes, high cheekbones, muscular neck and blond buzz cut hair. His unappeased cock pulsed in his pants. He gestured for the driver to roll down the window.

Matt looked into the dark, Germanic state trooper's face and went into a muted shock. He'd always considered himself a pretty big guy at six-foot-one,190, but compared to the man standing by his door, he felt like a pencil-necked geek. This cop wasn't merely big, but *hulking*. Easily six-five and 250 pounds. Or more. His chest was at least fifty-five inches wide, tapering down to a lean, hard stomach. The guy was all muscle underneath his Mounties-style uniform, and despite Matt's nervousness, his cock was starting to harden in his jeans.

He cleared his throat. "Good evening, officer."

"Sir," the trooper growled. "I clocked you driving seventy

miles-per-hour in a fifty-five zone. May I see your license, registration and insurance card please?"

Matt passed the requested documents and the PBA card to the cop.

"Have you been drinking this evening?" Faraway studied the license, then the youth.

"No, sir." Matt hoped his lust wasn't obvious; he didn't want to provoke the cop into doing anything homophobic.

"Wait here, son." Faraway headed for his cruiser and accessed the computer while adjusting his genitals. The kid's record popped up on the monitor. The two-year-old DUI made Faraway angry. He had little tolerance for rich college boys with no respect for the law. There had been times during his police career where he'd accepted blowjobs from these hot young punks looking for a break, but never with anyone driving under the influence.

And what's this?

He studied the Policeman's Benevolent Association card and the signature of the trooper who'd issued it: Frank Testaverde. Faraway smiled as he decided how to play this. He slipped the boy's papers into his tunic pocket and approached the Mustang.

"Sir, could you step out of the car?"

Heart pounding, Matt slowly exited his car with an undiminished hard-on. The roller lights and searchlight glare of the trooper's prowler blinded him, momentarily confusing his senses. Faraway noticed Matt's trouser trout with an inner smile. He ordered the young man to stand at the back of the vehicle with his hands on the trunk and said:

"Sir, by law, I must request permission to search your vehicle."

"Go ahead." Matt was getting pissed and, at the same time, uncharacteristically turned on by the man's complete dominance over the situation.

"Sir, are you concealing any drugs, contraband or weapons in your vehicle?" Faraway enjoyed the way the young man was hiding his angst behind a tough-boy mask.

"Nope. Look around. Just don't trash my car."

Faraway gave the interior a cursory search and found nothing suspicious. He strode around to the trunk and ordered Matt to open it. A large duffel bag, spare tire and tire jack kit were the only things inside.

"What's in the bag, son?"

"Hockey gear."

"Step to the side of the car, son, and place your hands on the roof."

"Am I under arrest?" Matt started to worry.

"No, son, but I am going to search you. Standard procedure." Faraway lied. "Please turn around and place your hands on the roof."

Matt placed his hands on the roof of his Mustang, but not before noticing a large lump in Faraway's baggy pants. He was shocked and excited, but also unwilling to risk pissing off the cop.

"Up against the car." The trooper used his body to press Matt against the passenger door of the Mustang. Matt's hardened cock mashed against the metal door as his ass cheeks registered the presence of a very large cop dick pressing against his lower back. A chill went down Matt's spine right to his balls. The cop's large hands did a quick and professional search of Matt's body, patting down his chest to his stomach and crotch with fluid grace. The hands brushed across Matt's erect cock for a moment, then headed due south, down his thighs, calves, ankles and up again to his ass.

There was a pause, followed by a hard double-palmed smack to Matt's buttocks, causing his ass to hitch in the air as his dick dribbled in his boxer briefs. The cop then inserted his booted leg between Matt's calves. "Spread 'em," the man ordered, forcing Matt's right leg farther open. The trooper reached under Matt's pits and across his chest again, then down his abs near the front of his jeans. Matt knew that this search was overly thorough and downright indiscreet, but he didn't care. The trooper's hands caressed against the lump in Matt's jeans, then slipped underneath his T-shirt across the naked skin of his back. Matt flinched as the cop's rough palms grazed his smooth skin, then abruptly withdrew.

Faraway stepped back, his dick standing at full attention. "Stay here, sir," he ordered. "Hands where I can see 'em." He moved to the trunk and opened the hockey bag. The musky scent of leather and sweat filled his nostrils as his hands pawed around inside its contents. He pulled out the boy's jock and felt the dampness on his fingertips. He replaced the jock and heard glass clinking within the bag. He dug deeper and found an unopened champagne bottle.

"What is this, son?"

"What does it look like?" Matt said with an ersatz bravado he didn't feel.

"Do not mouth off to me. You have a previous DUI on your record. The presence of liquor in your vehicle is not a good sign."

"It's still sealed, sir. I haven't had anything to drink."

"Can you explain why it's in your bag?"

"I'm on the hockey team. Tonight was the semis. If we hadn't choked, that bottle would be empty and I wouldn't be here."

"Lost, huh?" Faraway replaced the bottle and shined his flashlight into the boy's eyes. "All right. You seem clean." There was a pause, then: "One other question. You gave me a PBA card issued by Frank Testaverde. What is your relationship with Trooper Testaverde?"

Matt hesitated. Testaverde was a sexy Italian officer with a penchant for hot young jocks. Matt had heard rumors about his sexual forays from other gay jocks in school. Most of the guys had expressed disappointment after discovering that the hot Guido state trooper was the exact opposite of an aggressive top, but being a top himself, Matt didn't mind. He'd speared the Italian stallion on numerous occasions and Testaverde had gifted him with the PBA card.

"Just friends," Matt told Faraway.

"Friends. What kind of friends?"

"What's this all about?"

"I think honesty would be your best policy right now. What kind of friends?"

"Close friends, okay?"

"Close friends," asked Faraway, "or intimate friends?"

"Why don't you ask Officer Testaverde?"

"I don't need to." Faraway said. "I've already fucked him—plenty of times. I still do when he isn't getting high-sticked in his crease by a smart-ass hockey player. Sir, I am issuing you a summons for speeding."

"Oh fuck! C'mon, man! My insurance is already through the roof! My Dad will murder me!"

Faraway didn't reply.

"Look, I'm really sorry, okay? How was I supposed to know you and Frank were hooked up? Please, man!"

"Testaverde and I are not an item and never were," said Faraway.

"I've had a fucking awful night. Can't you cut me some slack?"

"That is a possibility. I haven't radioed in any particulars about this stop."

"What do you want from me?"

"I think you know what I want."

Matt reached out, his hand shaking, and gently handled the cop's hard cock through his uniform pants. He had no qualms about playing with the cop, but he was also nervous and out of his league. Being a butch top that gave no quarter, he had never allowed anyone to dominate his play on or off the ice. But now he had no choice.

Faraway pushed Matt's hand away, then reached inside his chest pocket and produced Matt's papers. "You'll get these if you do exactly what I tell you to. Do you understand?"

Matt nodded.

"Get in your car and follow me. A mile up, I'm going to slow down and make a right. There's a utility road. Follow me. And no tricks. Your car may be fast, but mine is faster."

Matt followed the trooper's Caprice. A mile up the road, the brake lights flashed, then signaled for a right turn. Matt followed it along the graveled utility road. The moon vanished behind soaring clouds, leaving the whole expanse of dark land devoid of lights or any signs of life. He was nervous, yet intensely turned-on and electrically alive. The trooper came to a stop and cut his lights. Matt shut off his headlights and engine and waited. Soon he heard the crunch of boots on loose gravel. The footsteps stopped next to his door. Faraway's large frame was a dim silhouette in the night.

"Out of the car, son. You know the routine."

Matt did *not* know "the routine," but exited the car anyway. The hulking shape loomed before him, grabbed him roughly and manipulated him to the rear end of the Caprice. Matt's fight-or-flight reflexes were revved up like crazy as he was forced against the trunk. The cop released him.

"Turn around," he ordered.

Matt faced the policeman with a dry mouth and throbbing balls.

"Strip."

Matt stared at the cop, unsure of what to do next.

"There's no need to be coy, son. You know as well as I do that you want it. Now you're going to get it."

Matt pulled off his jacket and removed his shirt, shoes and pants and stood before the trooper in his boxer briefs. The cop walked up and abruptly yanked them down to his feet, causing Matt's eight-inch hard-on to slap against his stomach. Satisfied, the trooper used his boot to remove the underwear from Matt's feet, then guided his naked prisoner to the front quarter panel of his cruiser and gave him a rough slap on the ass. "Don't move," he ordered, then stepped back to the driver's side door and opened it. He removed his gun belt and threw it into his cruiser. He slammed the door shut and growled at the sight of the boy's lean body, hard with muscle, like a young grunt fresh out of boot camp. He hooked his mitts under the hockey player's armpits and easily lifted the youth up and laid him down on the hood. He stroked the boy's dick, all the while watching his face.

Matt couldn't stop trembling. His backside was warmed by the engine underneath the hood of the cruiser, but the rest of his body was shivering in the cool night air. He'd had plenty of erotic experiences, but all of them paled in comparison. The cop pinched Matt's left nipple forcefully. The unexpected pain and pleasure made Matt's lower back arch. The trooper pushed him back down and teased his cock tip with his rough fingers, spreading Matt's precum over the lower part of his shaft.

"You are mine," the cop growled. He licked Matt's neck and ears, nibbled on his nipples with his teeth. Matt raised his hands to touch Faraway's body, only to have them pinned down again. "Lie still. I'm in charge here." Faraway swallowed Matt's cock in one gulp. Matt's senses were scrambled. The unexpected pleasures the cop was eliciting from him had blown away his usual defenses. Faraway sensed the boy was on the verge of busting a nut and broke his lip lock. He pinched Matt's nipple, eliciting the desired groan. "You'll shoot when I want you to, boy."

Faraway forced an arm underneath Matt's thighs and raised them up into the air, then inserted his left thumb into the boy's bunghole.

"You feel that in your ass? That ass belongs to me now."

He unplugged his thumb, lowered the boy's legs, leaned down and swallowed his dick again. This time he sucked him true, keeping the youth's body locked with his arms as his mouth churned up a load in the boy's balls. He sensed Matt was getting ready to shoot. At the last moment he jacked him with his fist and watched as the writhing young man shot load after load on his own belly and chest, moaning and making the hood beneath them rumble. When the last of the boy's convulsions were over, Faraway released the youth.

Matt sat up and watched as Faraway removed his tunic and shirt, revealing a large rack of chiseled muscle underneath a sexy thatch of chest hair. A Marine Corps Devil Dog tattoo leered in the moonlit night from the trooper's upper left arm. Matt had seen plenty of big jocks in his time, but they were nothing compared to this muscular lethal weapon undressing before him. The cop placed the shirt inside his cruiser and grabbed his personal valise. He snapped it open and removed a tiny tube of lube and a condom. Then he grabbed a rag and slapped the door shut. "Clean yourself up." Faraway threw the rag at him and unscrewed the bottle of lube.

Matt wiped himself down with what was obviously a used cum rag. "Sir, I've never been fucked before," he said, taking note of the bottle of lube. "I don't know if—"

"Shut up and stand up. I'm not interested in your past. Right now you have a debt to work off."

The boy slid into a standing position. Faraway spun him around and gently knocked him forward so that he was bent over the edge of the hood. Faraway unzipped his pants and dropped them down over his high boots. He smacked his ten-inch dick on Matt's hairless buttocks. "You got a nice tight ass, son," he said while unfolding a condom over his cock. "I'm gonna break it in." He lubed up his thumb and plugged it into Matt's unwilling ass. The boy cried out loud and Faraway smacked his ass cheek. He pulled his thumb out, re-lubed it and plugged the boy again. He slipped some more lube over his latex-sheathed cock. When he had his dick thoroughly slicked, he kicked Matt's legs wide and spread his ass cheeks open with his hands.

Matt was terrified. Faraway's cock was huge and he'd barely been able to tolerate so much as the cop's thumb in his ass! He cried out as the trooper seated his dickhead on his ring. He squeezed his ass shut, but the trooper reached underneath him and pinched his nipple. His ass-chute unexpectedly released and was wedged open as the cop's dickhead popped into his sphincter. Matt shifted his body on the hood of the cop's prowler, seeking escape, but Faraway held him down, anticipating each of Matt's attempts at freedom with an all-too-effective countermove. The cop pinched his nipple again and slipped more dick meat into him. Lost in the intensity, Matt dimly realized the moans and groans he heard were coming from his own lips. The ex-Marine slapped the boy's ass cheek, distracting him from the pain deep in his ass.

"Shut up and take it like a man."

The trooper forced another inch inside. Matt's body started to buck, making the Caprice's hood rumble beneath him. His trapped cock started to harden as the cop's cock massaged his prostate. There was pain, agony even, but this sudden pleasure was totally unexpected. He thought he'd understood everything there was to know about sexual dominance. But now, with this state trooper's ten-inch python snaking into his guts, he realized he had some unlearning to do now that *he* was on the receiving end of a grudge fuck. Mixed with his pain and shame was a deeply erotic physical and psychological pleasure that blew away all resistance, forcing him to submit mind and body to the cop's sexual intent. He panted as the trooper seated the last of his ten inches into him and suddenly became completely immobile.

Faraway bent over until his chest was on the boy's back. "Relax. I'm gonna stay like this until you get used to it, okay?" He placed his arms over Matt's and interlocked their fingers together. "You have a terrific body, Matt. The moment I first laid eyes on you, I knew I had to have it." Faraway felt the boy's ass-chute alternately tense and tighten around his cock. "Give in to me, Matt. I'm not gonna hurt you. I want you to enjoy this. Just relax and submit."

Matt felt his taut muscles slowly unknotting themselves as he became accustomed to the cop's meat buried deep inside him. Faraway caressed his neck and ear lobes with the softest kisses and Matt became completely submissive, enjoying the large man's every move. The sudden switch from aggression to passion from this hard-ass was an unexpected thrill. The cop's massive body kept him warm against the chilly night, on him and in him, licking him, muttering appreciative words of passion and massaging his body with the subtle flexing of hard muscle. The cop withdrew his cock several inches and reseated it deep inside Matt.

"Just relax. Don't fight me, give in to me."

Faraway raised himself into a standing position and locked his hands around Matt's hips. He wanted to break the boy in slowly, but his pace quickened. Tenderness took a back seat; primal lust took over. He was no longer a state trooper or ex-Marine, no longer Alan Faraway, but some primordial beast lost in the sensual rhythm of raw sex and the gluttonous satisfaction of taking pleasure from another with animal force: hunter and hunted, locking in on his prey, taking it down with superior strength and training. Nostrils flared, grunting with each thrust, he rode the boy relentlessly, growling and sweating, pistoning with complete savagery. With a guttural roar, he slammed his body down on the boy and shot. And shot again. He locked his arms around Matt's rib cage and held him in an intense and powerful embrace. His hips still bucking, he shot again.

Regaining his senses in stages, he cupped Matt's ramrod into his fist. With his hard-on still deeply planted in Matt's ass, he massaged the young hockey player's prostate with his dickhead. The boy's body became rigid. Matt let out a deep roar of ecstasy and shot one ropey strand of jizz after another on the side of the prowler. As he did, Faraway held the exhausted boy against his body and whispered in his ear: "You are mine."

Matt woke the next morning in his parents' house, now understanding what his buddy Steve meant by that "freshly fucked feeling." Despite losing both the semi-finals and his virginity in the last 12 hours, he felt pretty good. Last night while dressing, Faraway had expressed a desire to meet again when a sudden radio call for assistance abruptly ended their night. Matt had no idea if he would ever see the cop again or what was to become of his fledgling hockey career, but at this moment, he felt relaxed and sated and simply didn't care.

"Hey, Matt?" It was his dad, pounding on the door. "You alive in there?"

"Yeah, Dad."

His father entered the room and regarded his son with a curious eye. "Your Mom and I missed ya after the game last night."

"It was losing and all. I guess you're kind of disappointed, huh?"

"Hell, no! The scouts were all over us last night and have been calling all morning."

"Scouts?"

He handed Matt a stack of phone messages.

"No shit," Matt thumbed through the stack.

"You sound surprised. You shouldn't be. We're proud of you."

Matt stared at the numbers and messages. One message in particular:

I HAVE SOMETHING YOU MIGHT WANT BACK. FARAWAY.

He read it again, then realized his father was still standing there. "Thanks, Dad."

"Get dressed and go apologize to your Mom."

"Yes, sir." Matt waited until his father was gone, then reached for his jacket slung over the TV. Sure enough, his license, registration, insurance and PBA cards were missing from his wallet. Faraway had never returned them when they hastily parted ways last night. He rose gingerly from the bed and picked up the phone. Faraway answered on the third ring.

"Good afternoon, sir. It's Matt. You have something of mine?"

"Yep. But to get it back, you've gotta earn it."

Matt's cock was already stirring. "Was that by accident or design?"

"Come over tonight and find out."

Faraway gave Matt directions, then, before hanging up, added:

"Oh, and Matt, a little advice from your friends at the State Patrol: drive carefully."

The Boy Who Read Bataille

SIMON SHEPPARD

Because he was actually French, he stood out in the class. That, and because he was gorgeous.

The class was Transgressive French Literature, otherwise known as Kink Lit 101. It was a popular one at my grad school. We got to read all the really twisted stuff: de Sade, Genet, Bataille. And Philippe was always a standout in class, not having to struggle to translate things. After all, it's not so easy to find the translation of "cocksucking motherfucking fag" in your *Larousse Dictionnaire Bilingue.*

I was attracted to him—I'm guessing everybody in the class was, both male and female—but he never gave a clue as to where his interests lay. His sexual interests, anyway. It was quite clear that as a reader he loved the thoroughly filthy works of Georges Bataille.

"God," he said one night, when a few of us—me, him, Ben, and Mary Anne—were polishing off a pesto pizza at Vito's, "I could just read *The Story of the Eye* over and over again."

"Really?" I said. I was more inclined toward Genet, who didn't seem to always be straining to shock.

"*Oui*. Ah, Bataille. The scene with the piss and the wardrobe? *Magnifique*. And I especially like the part where Simone breaks raw eggs with her ass."

I was glad he wasn't fixated on the scene with Sir Edmond at the bullfight, or the one with Marcelle's eyeball in Simone's vagina. Eeewww!

"I'd love," he continued, "to try that out."

"Yeah?" I was excited, but cagey. I looked at his smooth, pretty face, which nearly always wore a quizzical, almost distant expression, eyes lively but remote behind his glasses, his countenance crowned by a shock of dark brown hair.

"Oh God!" said Mary Anne. "Not me! That's gross."

"But you're taking a class on transgressive literature," said Ben. "Lighten up."

"Just because I read *Macbeth*," Mary Anne said, "doesn't mean I want to kill a king."

Good retort, but my mind was elsewhere, wondering how Philippe, body obviously well-knit even when he was fully clothed, would look naked, sitting in a bathtub full of raw eggs. I finished off my pesto pizza and followed the procession to the cash register, the picture of his slick-wet butt still throbbing in my mind.

Once outside the restaurant, I managed to send Ben and Mary Anne on their way without arousing suspicion and it wasn't long before Philippe and I were alone, walking toward his place. The four of us had polished off a couple of pitchers of beer, so I'll blame what I said next on intoxication:

"You really meant that? About the eggs?"

Philippe didn't look at me, just somewhere off in the distance, and he seemed a bit nervous when he nodded. "Very much, yes," he said, though he sounded uncertain. "Why?"

"Because ..." And then I hesitated, drunkenly tongue-tied.

Philippe helped me out. "Would you like to try something like that? With me?"

I couldn't say I'd ever considered it before. In fact, I wasn't sure how committed I was to it even then. Kink had never been my thing, not even in my masturbation fantasies, which generally centered on smooth-bodied guys bending over to show me their butt holes. But if this was my big chance to see Philippe with his clothes off, maybe even touch him ...

I nodded.

Soon we were gathering groceries at an all-night supermarket, my hard-on visible, I guess, to anyone who'd bothered to look. What the hell, transgressive is transgressive, right?

It wasn't a long walk back to Philippe's, but it seemed endless. He lived on the third floor, but I swear there were nine flights of stairs. Once we were inside his small, grad-student-cluttered living room, we set our bags on the coffee table. Awkward silence. Without a word, he stripped down to his undershirt and jeans. Then, never looking me straight in the eye, he slowly peeled down his jeans.

I'd never seen anything so ostentatiously perfect as Philippe standing there in just his undershirt. Slightly stocky and broad-shouldered, he didn't look like the kind of guy who'd want to discuss Derrida. His soft dick had a long, luxurious foreskin. His thighs were creamy white, muscular, perfectly shaped, amazing.

And then he turned around.

I've seen plenty of asses in my young life, but Philippe's was a Greek god's ass, a Michaelangelo-statue ass, the ass of the Heavenly Host. It was, quite frankly, the best ass I'd ever seen. Philippe sauntered over to the bags on the table and pulled out the plastic shower curtains he'd bought. He tore open the package and, with the nonchalant attitude of someone decorating the high school gym for a prom, laid the curtains on the floor, keeping his back toward me. He *must* have been aware of the effect his astonishing, creamy ass had on those lucky enough to behold it. As he bent over to spread out the plastic, his pure white butt cheeks parted just enough to let me see a thin line of dark hair around the hole. I almost came in my pants.

With the floor covered in vinyl, he strolled over to the table again, his butt cheeks shifting with every step, and unloaded the grocery bags: two cartons of 18 extra-large eggs, a bottle of chocolate syrup, tins of vanilla pudding, spray cans of whipped cream.

"Are you ready?" he asked, turning to face me, his eyes quizzical behind his owlish glasses.

Turn around so I can see your ass again, I wanted to reply. Instead, I said, "Yes."

"And you want to do this? Really?"

I unbuttoned my fly and pulled out my hard cock. "See?" I said. "Now get down on all fours, okay?"

"Sorry," he said, nearly knocking his glasses off as he pulled his undershirt over his head, revealing a flurry of armpit hair, "I guess I'm a bit nervous."

"Well, it's my first time, too. On the floor, okay?" I really wanted to be a badass, kinky motherfucker, but as I stood there with my big, stupid hard-on jutting from my pants, watching Philippe getting on his knees and then all fours, I just felt shy. If Bataille or de Sade or Genet had been watching, they would have thought: Pathetic! Or *Pathetique!*

"Well?" Philippe's voice was giving nothing away.

"Can I, um, touch you first?"

"Of course."

So I got down on my knees, just behind him, next to the pure European beauty of his ass, and extended a tentative hand. He flinched a bit at my touch, then relaxed as I stroked the cheek, ran my hand over its classical curves, then gently trailed two fingers down the crack, and traced down from the tailbone till I felt the soft warmth of his hole. With my other hand I reached between his lean thighs, brushing his pendulous ball-sac, then aimed upward till I grabbed his dick. It was gratifyingly stiff, but the generous foreskin still covered the head; I slid it back and forth over the moist head-flesh as my other hand massaged his hole.

"*Les oeufs* ..." Philippe said. He was sounding impatient. I wanted to fuck him and he was thinking about groceries. The eggs. Damn this kink stuff.

Reluctantly I got up, walked over to the table and opened an egg carton. The white shell was slightly cool in my hand. I cracked it on the edge of the table.

"Ready?" I asked, like something momentous was about to happen.

He looked up at me, straight at me through those horn-rimmed glasses and smiled. "*Oui.*"

I stood above him and pulled the shell apart, letting the raw goo drop onto the smooth, white flesh of his ass. I wanted it to drip right down the crack, but my aim was a bit off. Philippe muttered something in French.

"Pardon?" I said.

"I was reciting Bataille." He paused, then began again, apparently having memorized the bit leading up to Marcelle's suicide. The guy was amazingly weird. But his ass was amazingly fantastic. I got another egg, cracked it, and, holding it close to his flesh, hit the target, the yolk oozing right down his ass crack. I spit in my hand and worked my throbbing dick for a minute while I watched raw egg slithering down his thighs and onto the plastic-covered floor.

"Oh, fuck," I said. And meant it.

Then I went back to the table and picked up the first egg carton. Sixteen left. Standing above him, I dropped the eggs one-by-one onto Philippe, onto his shoulders, the small of his back, but especially onto his wonderful, wonderful ass.

By the time I'd gone through most of the carton, the place was a mess and Philippe was thoroughly covered with viscous whites and bright streaks of yolk. I was about to suggest that we'd made enough mess, when he reached back with both hands and pulled his ass cheeks wide apart. His deep pink asshole gleamed beneath a raw egg glaze: boypussy *tartare*. I dropped to my knees, right between his kneeling legs, stuck my face into his sloppy-wet ass, and started lapping at his high-cholesterol hole. He paused in his recitation of Bataille long enough to say "Fuck, yeah" and back up against my tongue. I reared back again, reached for an egg, and smashed it into his open hole. I was— and my oozing cock agreed—beginning to really enjoy this.

The chocolate syrup was next. I stood over Philippe for a moment, looking down at his egg-slick ass, beauty in its slippery and wet mess. Then I opened the nozzle of the bottle and let a drizzle of dark-brown syrup fall onto his wet, white skin. If this was the final exam for the Transgressive Lit class, I had a feeling I was passing with flying colors.

I squeezed the bottle and a stream of sweet syrup hit his hole, drenching egg whites, yolks, and bits of shell. It was beautiful, that hole, those food-covered butt cheeks. As beautiful as his ass had been when it was clean and white, it was even sexier all sullied and filthy with food. I wanted to fuck it. And I *was* going to fuck his ass. It's why I'd slipped a package of Trojans into the grocery basket.

The syrup bottle sputtered to emptiness. I dropped it, picked up the whipped cream and shook hard. With a flourish, I topped the egg-and-chocolate slop with swirls of whipped cream, shooting a big white rosette right on Philippe's asshole. He took his hands away and his cheeks came together, squeezing out a big glob of chocolate cream. I ran my fingers up the crack of his messy ass and brought them, all covered with brownish goop, to my lips. Sweet.

But my cock demanded attention. I found the rubbers and tore the packet open with my teeth, my slippery fingers straining to get a grip on the foil.

"What are you doing?" Philippe asked. I glanced his way. He was looking up at me through those glasses of his, expression vague as ever. It was a stupid question.

"What does it look like? I'm putting on a rubber."

"No." Just that, sounding the same in English or French. No.

While I hesitated, wondering if all the work I'd done still

wouldn't get me into Philippe's butt, he rose to his knees. He grabbed his dick with his goo-covered hand and jacked his foreskin back and forth over his swollen, shiny cock head. Looking somewhere in the room, but not at me, never at me, his face scrunched up in lust.

"Oh, yeah ... oh, yeah ... oh, yeah," he chanted. His glasses were sliding down his sweaty nose.

If I'd been smart, I guess I would have gotten behind him and at least stuck my fingers up his ass. Maybe even my dick. But I wasn't smart. I was polite. I just stood there gaping as Philippe shot a big load of sperm, gush after gush, onto the swamp of eggs, chocolate, and cream.

"That's it," Philippe said, recovering quickly. "You can wash up in the kitchen sink. I'm going to go shower."

I didn't know what to say. "Fuck you, asshole" came to mind, but when I thought about how gorgeous his asshole actually looked ...

By the time I'd rinsed my hands and stuffed my still semi-hard cock back into my pants, the shower was already running. I went into the bathroom to say good-bye. There behind a clear plastic curtain, the French boy was washing his butt. He spread his cheeks, soaped himself up and drew small wet circles on his hole. My dick stretched to full hardness again.

"Philippe?"

He turned. Amazingly, he still had his glasses on. He didn't say a word. I'd been dismissed, my part in his little literary experiment apparently at an end. He'd had his transgressive fun.

When I left Philippe's, the door locked itself behind me with a click.

Butt Brigade

TROY STORM

"Okay, you burr-cut buttheads," the platoon sergeant bellowed, "turn around, drop 'em and polish 'em up for inspection!"

We obeyed, half asleep and grumbling under our breaths at being routed out of the sack at the crack of dawn, though we were pretty much used to being treated like shit by this world-famous military academy in its determination to build our character—or break us. We staggered to the foot of our bunks, turned our backs to the wide aisle separating the two rows of beds, shoved our khaki boxers down to our ankles and stood tall, naked butts pimpling in the cold.

Another pair of boots clunked along with Sarge's as he strolled down the center of the barracks inspecting our asses. Occasionally there would be the sound of a hard slap on a bare bottom or a quiet comment like, "Nice morning boner, cadet." But other than that, we just waited through it and tried not to yawn. When Sarge got to the other end of the barracks, he told us to cover and about face. We pulled up our shorts and turned around. He was alone. Whoever was with him had gone.

"Okay, you goose-bumped sorry asses, those of you who were anointed by my callused palm report to my quarters. The rest of you losers hit the showers."

There were six of us. All with outstanding backsides.

"One of our fine officers—along with me—is a prime buttman," Sarge told us once we were lined up in his private quarters. "You have been selected as candidates for the Butt Brigade, meaning your asses are possibly worthy of appreciation. If you wish to participate in the Butt Brigade on a completely unofficial extra-curricular basis, you will be expected to put up with appalling humiliation and will in return, receive awesome sexual gratification. Any takers?"

We all stared at Sarge. Six weeks with no privacy and too worn out to jerk off, all of us were instantly on the alert. Boxers tented.

The sergeant smiled. "Anybody with moral or religious objections is free to go, no questions asked."

Sadly, Peterson, a man with a truly set of boss buttocks, raised his hand. So did Macardy. Sarge nodded and they left the room.

Four of us remained: Raymr, a cute black guy with a shaved head who was built like a glazed-brick shithouse and had an ass on him that was hard to contain even inside his loose school-issued boxers; Waterford, a blond Southern stud who probably

could strip a cotton plant if it got caught in the rock-hard glob-
ular vise of his tight tush; Fleish, a bespectacled, jet-black curly-
haired Jewish guy with the biggest dick I had ever seen on a kid
and an asshole that looked like an oil funnel; and me, Bradley, a
blue-eyed, brown-haired Irish hunk (if I say so myself) with the
hottest set of as-yet-unbreached gluteus maximi on our high
school football team.

I wasn't sure who swung which way—and since nobody
was asking, nobody was telling—but we all sure as hell had a
look on our faces that showed we were game for whatever Sarge
and his buddy could shovel our way.

The initial inspection of the Butt Brigade took place a couple of days later, again in Sarge's quarters, which were kinda
cramped. The rest of the platoon had been split up into a bunch
of units and sent on its way to classes and drills. That way, none
of the other guys were ever quite sure when the BB was getting
its workout. Turned out the major was the officer who had been
with Sarge when we were picked. He was in Sarge's quarters now,
naked except for the hat pulled low on his head, dark aviators
and a pair of shiny dog tags gleaming against his chiseled pec-
torals. He was built lean and mean, a hot-looking stud with one
of the most mouth-watering rear ends I had ever seen on a
grown man—not that I had had the pleasure of seeing all that
many—and I couldn't wait to be butt searched by him.

We grabbed our ankles for the major. He flicked our butt
cheeks lightly with a riding crop, which brought them flinching
to attention, and inspected our holes by poking at them with the
leather whip. Fleish, the guy with the funnel-shaped asshole, had
a nice pair of buns—tight cantaloupes with a wide crack

between 'em. His hole was like the entrance to a hidden mine, open, moist and funneling down into a dark tunnel.

The major and Sarge bent low. The major poked in the end of the riding crop. It kept going ... and going. "Hol—lee ..." Sarge paused. The major switched ends and pushed in the leather handle. Fleish shoved his glasses back up on his nose and smirked. The major and Sarge leaned in closer to watch ... six inches, eight inches, almost a foot of the crop disappear into Fleish's butt.

The major wiggled the leather probe around and Fleish went from a half hard-on to a boner that had us all staring. Ten fucking inches on a fucking five-foot-seven, 18 year-old kid is quite a sight. Sarge looked as stunned as the rest of us. The major looked like he had discovered the Holy Grail. There went my quick promotion, I thought.

The major, who had worked up a damn decent wrist-sized eight with a big purple mushroom head—just the kind of butt probe to make my virgin asshole twinge with anticipation—pulled Fleish upright, put his arm around the kid's shoulder and led him off to Sarge's bunk. The riding crop stuck up Fleish's tight little ass whipped back and forth as he sauntered away.

To conceal his metal bed, Sarge had hung a sheet in front of it for a little privacy. The threadbare cotton was stained and wrinkled. Sarge would never make a good wife. But he sure as hell was intent on making a good husband.

"Line up, pretty asses," he growled. We lined up. "Feel free to hand off a load or two." He distributed condoms, which we dutifully donned. "Turn around and pay me no mind." We turned around, but we sure as hell paid attention where attention was due. Sarge dropped to his knees and went from butt to butt, snuffling our cracks and slapping our cheeks with sharp, open-palm pops that didn't so much hurt as raise the level of acceptance of what he was planning to do.

"Damn, Sarge, that's a fucking turn-on." Raymr, the black dude, leaned forward and gave Waterford and me a sly grin as he put his hands on his thighs and let Sarge do what he was doing. Sarge worked his face inside the polished mahogany mountains for a while until the Raymr looked like he was going to pass out from happiness. Then Sarge moved on to Waterford.

The big blond looked a little worried as Sarge wormed his chin in between the Southern boy's ripened and readies to slurp away at his crack. The kid's eyes popped and rolled back in his head as he pounded his pud with both fists while Sarge suctioned up his hole. Waterford came in about five seconds, spraying a load that impressed both Raymr and me. Then it was my turn.

I had never had a rim job before, though I had dreamt about it after practically memorizing the lip and tongue action of the Butt Luv videos I had hidden away in my closet at home. Sarge's rough tongue trilled over my tightly clenched anal entry. My asshole knew what was coming. Maybe not right away (though the grunts and curses from behind the sheet made me believe the major wasn't the kind of guy to be put off when he wanted to drill butt), but sooner or later I was going to get fucked and as much as I looked forward to my dream date, my butt hole wasn't so sure.

Sarge treated me like I was a worthwhile challenge to his talented tongue. He swabbed my hole down, drenching it in hot saliva, then twirled around the tender trapdoor with the tip of his flickering mouth organ until all the nerve endings surrounding my sphincter were St. Vitusing with pleasure. He backed off and cultivated the surrounding territory, licking and lapping at my cheeks. He polished the spittle with his palms until I could imagine the pink globes glowing with a fine, hot fire. I had good-looking, well-rounded butt cheeks. Many's the time I had gotten my rocks off watching their firm flawless surfaces—except for maybe a bullshit pimple or two—shimmying as I wanked away.

Speaking of which, I was about to come. My dick was rock hard and throbbing, my nuts tight and ready to blow. I tugged on my tits as Sarge lip-loved my love mounds and when I felt the flow coming, I pinched the hell out of my nips. Dick cream gushed into the rubber. It was only after I stood there a couple of minutes jerking and shooting, feeling my whole body tingling and shimmering from Sarge's loving tongue, that I realized the asshole had rammed a finger up my asshole.

My sphincter hated it, my prostate loved it. My rectum reserved opinion. Since I wasn't in total pain, I couldn't care the hell less. My bone had blasted a very respectable load, my nipples were singing and my butt cheeks were glowing. I shot more stuff into the latex tube until the tip hung off the end of my drooping dick, swaying with a satisfying heft.

The major staggered out from behind the curtain, looking well pleased, his drooping, rubber-covered dick dripping butt juice. He was soon followed by a goofy-looking Fleish, his ten inches still standing proud, walking like he was going to walk funny for the next few hours.

"Take care of the kid, Sergeant," the major instructed. Sarge pulled off his pants and pushed Fleish back behind the sheet.

"Boys, I don't want to show favorites," the major said, pulling on a fresh rubber, "so I'm planning to fuck you all before this session is finished."

He placed Raymr's hands on the top of Sarge's beat-up chest of drawers, kicked the guy's legs apart and then hoisted his own semi-soft and stroked it into a fully-loaded, red-nosed cannon, which he positioned between the gleaming black ovals of Raymr's ass. Raymr's glutes tensed into cut crescents as the major pressed forward. The private's full, moist lips opened soundlessly and his fingers gripped the battered wood of the ancient upright piece of furniture.

Waterford and I watched, mesmerized, as the latex-covered cylinder of the major's bone drove relentlessly into Raymr's ass. The black guy clenched his teeth, pounded the top of the chest and said: "Yeah, fucking, man, oh, fucking yeah, that is the way *home*."

Waterford grinned and I gulped. My butthole felt tighter than ever.

The major got about half his dick up Raymr's butt. He began to fuck the black hole, gently dragging his massive pole in and out. With a yell, Raymr came, his dick jerking and bouncing as the shots of pure white cream fired out of the glossy black shaft.

"Very nice, son, very nice." The major pulled out and patted Raymr's butt. Raymr's dark purple glutes jerked as he finished firing. He leaned onto the chest, resting his cheek bone on his quivering forearm, a silly grin on his face.

"Thank you, *sir*," he gasped. "I hope you'll do it again soon, *sir*. That was fucking *fiiiiine!*"

The major took on a satisfied look, and after pulling off the used one, rolled on another heavy duty condom. Waterford turned and grabbed the edge of the sergeant's desk, poking his butt out toward the major. The major shoved a couple of his strong fingers up Waterford's ass and when the Southern bitch took it without even grunting, the major shoved all five fingers in and reamed away.

Waterford arched his back and tilted his hips so that his rosy pink globes spread even farther apart. The major replaced his fingers with his dick and impaled Waterford with three-quarters of his massive ramrod before the young stud began to moan that he couldn't take any more. The major was a prime time gentleman fucker. He slid in and out slowly and steadily until Waterford was snickering and giggling and begging for a little rougher treatment, which the major segued into. Soon the Southern stud was spraying all over Sarge's desk as the major hosed out his hole.

Then it was my turn. I was feeling pretty good about how the other military whores had taken his cock without too many tears when I zeroed in on the major re-sheathing his honker. Damn thing must have grown with each butt busting. I swallowed and felt my ass go dry as the major put his hands on my hips.

"Cutest, hottest butt in the barracks, private." His whisper was hot against my cheek. "That's a beauty down there. I want to treat it right."

Oh ... well, gee ...

He treated my butt right, all right. Continuing with the loving Sarge had lavished on it, he tongued out my hole and sandpapered my butt cheeks with his afternoon stubble. A few minutes of slow and easy worship and I was feeling no fear. He eased inside me while lightly scratching at my butt cheeks with his fingernails and nibbling on my ear lobe. Wow. Weird being filled up from the outside in. My colon wasn't quite sure what to make of it. The major kept nibbling and rubbing and pushing in and soon my ass had gone from feeling weird to feeling wonderful.

By the time he had worked all of his huge honker into my butt, I had one happy hole. I begged him to give it to me hard, and the major, with a grunt of determination, set out to do just that. The other two guys, impressed with how my ass had swallowed all of the major's meat—and that I was still standing— moved around to get in on the action.

Raymr polished my tits and Waterford sucked me off as I reached back and grabbed the major's butt to help him drive his stake as deep inside my gulping hole as he could. His ass muscles flexed under my tight grip, his strongly-shaped glutes writhing like a nest of pythons trapped under the tough skin. The major blew out my butt as Waterford blew out my nuts and Raymr's pinching fingers blew out my tits. Sarge shoved back the sheet hiding his bunk when he heard all the commotion and we caught a glimpse of him squatting over Fleish as Fleish's load blew out Sarge's butt.

The next session we learned how to daisy butt fuck. Awesome. I made Private First Class before any of the other guys. Obviously I was born for the Butt Brigade.

Tony's Tasty Tail

PHILIP McKRACK

Some guys like eating ass because they know it drives another guy crazy in the sack. Others do it for the sheer joy of tasting juicy man ass. I fall under the latter category. Don't get me wrong. It definitely adds to the experience to hear a guy moaning with unbridled pleasure; but truth is, I wouldn't care if the dude was out cold. I'd still be slurpin' that tangy, puckering fruit till the cows come home.

As a bisexual, married man, the joy of rimming blindsided me. I had seen it done in videos and magazines, but the act always seemed repulsive. Just the thought of what comes out of an asshole is enough to turn anyone's stomach—well, unless, of course, you're into that sort of thing, which I am not (*not that there's anything wrong with that. Eweh!*).

The night of my awakening started at Rage in West Hollywood, the longstanding nightclub in the heart of

Boystown. It was only my second time at a gay club alone and I'm sure I looked a little apprehensive. Here I was, a half-straight black guy in a mostly non-black gay club, probably fidgeting and seeming pretty wet behind the ears.

Still, I must have not been too out of it because I noticed a guy across the room checking me out. He was only 5'2" but hotter 'n hell. He had olive skin, thick dark hair and the face of an angel. He also had the body of an Adonis, but they come a dime a dozen in WeHo. Before I knew it, he was standing beside me with two drinks in his hands.

"You look like you can use one of these," he said, and told me his name was Tony.

Tony was even more stunning close-up. He said he was an artist and had lots of his work on display in his apartment, which happened to be just around the corner. It wasn't long before we headed over to his place.

He had quite a setup. He was one of the guys who paints the oversized album covers displayed on the walls outside music stores. There was a humongous painting of Madonna over his bed. Janet Jackson, Cher and several other pop stars populated his apartment walls. After the tour, I had to pee and went to the bathroom. When I returned to the bedroom, he was lying face-down on the bed, nude except for a pair of those little white slouch socks made famous by *Flashdance*. He was moaning and wiggling on the big furry spread that was his bedcover. I was so turned on, I could hardly stand. Or was it that god-awful cocktail?

His ass was round and five shades paler than the rest of his body. His buns were like two perfect snow-white, velvety-smooth mounds. If it weren't for his beautiful crack, it would've looked like he was still wearing a pair of white briefs. The hair on his head was thick, but there wasn't one follicle anywhere on his backside. I leaned over the bed and started kissing the back of his neck. He promptly scooted forward until my lips were caressing the silky skin between his shoulder blades. Then he scooted up even more until I was kissing the small of his back, just north of his crack. He had two cute little dimples on either side of his spine. I kissed them both and could smell the musky scent of his crack. I had expected it would smell shitty, but it didn't. It smelled like man, fuckin' hot sexy man. I was turned on but apprehensive. He rotated his hips, purposely parting his crack and revealing the most tantalizing pucker I had ever laid eyes on. It reminded me of the eyelets on my grandma's lace tablecloth, only it was pink and winking at me.

"Come on man! Do it! Eat my hole!"

My head said "no," but my tongue was beginning to say "yes." I struck a deal with myself. I decided to just touch it with my lips to see what it felt like. I could always just go to the bathroom and scrub my mouth with soap and rubbing alcohol.

I kissed it once. It was like satiny candy to my lips. My repulsion was melting. His hips bucked, urging me on. I went back in for another peck, then another. Then he moaned, "I need your tongue up my ass!"

I decided to lick the inside of his butt cheeks and along his crack but nothing more. But once I got down there, his hand palmed the back of my head like a basketball and pushed my face deeper into his crevice. My tongue told my brain to take a hike and darted in and out of his hole like a bobbin on a sewing machine. He humped the bed and begged for more. I licked and gnawed and sucked on that hole as if it were my last meal. I sucked so hard, I think I caused a hemorrhoid to develop. I licked that, too.

When my tongue cramped, I lay on the bed and started jacking off. Before I could catch my breath, I looked up to see that ass descending on my face. "I hope you don't think you're finished eatin' my asshole," he warned me. "I'm gonna ride your face till I pop my wad all over your chest."

I was more than happy to oblige. I came first but didn't mind working Tony's tasty hole until he shot what seemed like a bucket of cum all over my chest and stomach.

I forgot to scrub my face that night. I still wonder if my wife smelled man-ass on my mug as I kissed her when I got home. She did kinda shoot me this funny look. I don't know. Maybe it was just my imagination.

Kenny's Ass

M. THOMAS

"Hey, kid, I hope they're paying you to do that!"
The strength of that voice across the schoolyard
touched something deep within me. I was banging together
blackboard erasers and standing in a white cloud of chalk dust.
I turned to see Kenny coming toward me, working a toothpick
in his mouth under his mustache. His handsome Mexican-
American face was smiling and his dark eyes bore into me. I was
afraid of saying something really stupid.

"I got the highest score on Sister Mary Margaret's spelling
quiz," I stammered, embarrassed by his interest and intense gaze.

"So you get to clean erasers instead of playing catch." He lit
a cigarette and exhaled two streams of blue smoke from his nostrils. "Keep up the good work and you'll be ready for a bank job
before you know it." He let out a kind, exuberant laugh.

An old guy—all of 30—Kenny was the best mechanic in

our neighborhood and one of the few people my dad let work on our cars. He worked at the garage owned by his father-in-law, Manny, and after Kenny's wife died in childbirth, leaving him widowed without any children, he became the son Manny and Manny's wife had never had.

My sister said Kenny was "cool," which put him right up there with James Dean, Dick Clark and President Kennedy. Kenny had wide shoulders, rich, short black hair, strong legs, muscled arms and an ass that could have been the inspiration for shrink-to-fit Levi's. I was only 14 and wasn't even jacking off yet. My biggest fantasy was spending a weekend at Disneyland. And still I knew that there was something special about Kenny's ass. The muscles in his butt moved when he danced weekend nights at the Domino Café. Women who came to the garage pointed at his ass and made comments in Spanish. A couple of the guys at the garage slapped him on the butt a lot. *Nalgas.* One of the first words of Spanish I learned. Butt.

"Stopping by today?" Kenny took one last drag on the cigarette, threw it to the ground and put it out with his foot. "We're working on a vintage vet."

"Straight after school," I promised. He smiled his big white smile, tussled my hair and kept on his way. I wanted to watch him leave, but the bell rang, so I clumsily grabbed my erasers and ran back into school.

My family was close with Manny's family and at first, I was pretty much just another kid hanging around the garage after school But after Kenny's wife passed away and he moved in with his in-laws, he and I became good buddies. Kenny and Manny and the guys never made me feel like just a kid, although sometimes, especially when a pretty woman came into the shop, they'd switch to Spanish and I'd hear some of the words that the older Mexican boys in the neighborhood used a lot. I didn't mind. My parents were from France and I only knew *poquito* Spanish. Still I felt like one of the boys.

Kenny and his crew did a lot of work for my dad and by the time I turned 17, I was spending most of my extra time at the garage. I guess I had grown up quite a bit because Kenny and his co-workers now spoke English when commenting on a female customer's breasts or ass or how a good fuck would put a certain woman in a better mood. They also talked a lot about eating pussy, getting blow jobs and fucking ass. Kenny, who'd won a bunch of medals during the Korean War, bragged about all the fine pussy he'd had on leave in Japan. Then he'd look at me and say stuff like: "Let me know when you you're ready to do more with your dick than take a piss. I'll set you up right, I promise."

I didn't know squat about pussy, but I'd already learned that my dick was good for a lot more than urinating. The Domino Café was our local restaurant and truck stop, and more than a few horny truckers had introduced me to the joys of being sucked off and taking a horny dick or two—or more—down my throat. I steered clear of the bulls, the more aggressive truckers who loved to fuck tight chicken ass. I was saving my cherry ass for a special occasion and was content with giving and getting head with my trucker friends until I graduated from high school.

When I turned 18, I started thinking more about Kenny's promise to find me some female action. These were the sex-drenched '60s and I would soon be leaving San Diego for college in Northern California. I was eager to explore the heterosexual side of sex, to find out if pussy could make my cock feel as good as a man's throat and ass. I finally decided to broach the subject with Kenny. I was nervous as hell and rambled on until Kenny decided to cut to the chase.

"You need some pussy, kid?" he said, looking up from the engine block he was working on. "I got a little party date next Friday night. Why don't you come with me? We can spend the night at a motel."

"What about my parents?"

"Tell 'em we're going camping. Don't worry about it."

When the big night finally arrived, Kenny and I had an early dinner with my family and he chatted with my folks about our camping trip, assuring them—adult to adult—everything was going to be fine. My dad smiled a lot. The coast was clear. My cherry would soon be history.

"Our party date is this chick I ball from Rosarita," Kenny said as he backed out of the driveway. "I got us a room in town for the night. We gotta go pick her up at her sister's place out in La Mesa. We'll play it by ear, okay, kid?"

He seemed almost as nervous as I was.

"What if she doesn't like me?" I asked.

"From the size of that hard-on you're throwing right now, I'd say you'd make any broad pretty damned happy. Besides, I'll be the one to get things going."

"So what's your friend like?"

"Pretty face, nice tits, nice ass. Her pussy's still pretty tight, considering all the cock she's had."

"Jeez, Kenny she's not—"

"Don't worry, kid. Mariana's a good broad who loves dick. Her old man can't get it up anymore. When's she wants to party, she gives Kenny a call. I don't see much wrong with a broad wanting a lot of cock. Some guys need a lot of pussy; nobody much cares about that."

"Doesn't she worry about getting pregnant?"

"Mariana can't have no more kids. She had her motor took out."

We pulled up to a large ranch-style house. A tall woman of about 30 hurried to the truck. I climbed out and let Mariana settle in between us. Mariana and Kenny chatted in Spanish. We drove to a nice motel not too far from the city's embarcadero. Kenny gave Mariana the room key, then pulled me back as she headed to the room and whispered, "She thinks you're cute. And she's heard that Jewish guys have special powers in the sack."

A few minutes later, the three of us were sitting on the edge of the bed, naked. Mariana pretended to be impressed by my limited Spanish. I didn't have to pretend to be impressed by her tits. We were drinking some of the good Mexican beer she had brought with her and before I knew it, Mariana and I were kissing and Kenny had cupped one of her tits and was licking at the nipple. Inspired and slightly loaded, I did the same with her other tit. Soon she was stroking both our cocks. Kenny worked a couple of fingers in and out of Mariana's shaved pussy, then spread her pussy lips wide and told me to take a look.

"This is what tonight's all about, kid." He gently pushed Mariana back onto the bed. "Just do what I do, and you'll be okay."

I felt light headed. The room began to swirl around the

focal point of Kenny's ass, bobbing up and down as he crawled onto the bed and ate Mariana's pussy. Kenny's ass. It had a life of its own. I stared at it and my dick began to throb. I knew what I wanted more than Mariana's pussy. I wanted to lick Kenny's ass-hole, to taste it, eat it, fuck it and worship those taut mounds of man flesh with my tongue, mouth and cock. I wanted to probe the depth of that beautiful ass. The rest of the night, it was Kenny's ass that kept my cock hard.

We fucked Mariana for a couple of hours. Kenny and I both unloaded in her mouth, on her tits, in her cunt and up her ass. Fucking Mariana was actually a lot of fun, but I don't remember much except Kenny's ass moving up and down in tight circles as he fucked her pussy. Kenny's ass moving in and out as he stood by the bed while Mariana sucked his big dark cock. Kenny's ass spread wide beneath him as Marina rode up and down on his cock. Kenny's ass swaying over Mariana's face as she sucked his cock while I pounded away at her pussy. Kenny's ass close enough to eat as he fucked Mariana's cunt over my face while she sucked her pussy juice off of my cock. Kenny's ass flexing as he shot his load on Mariana's upturned face. Kenny's ass is all I remember. That and his finger, briefly probing my asshole as I fucked Mariana doggy style. What was *that* about?

When Mariana headed into the bathroom to shower, Kenny sat next to me on the bed, nervous and lost in thought. I grabbed his pack of cigarettes from the nightstand and fetched us a smoke. When I reached over to light his cigarette, his hand cupped mine and our eyes met through the smoke .

"Well, kid, how ya doing?" He flashed a mischievous smile.

"Fucking great, just a little tired." I was thinking about

Kenny's ass and the finger he had shoved up my mine.

"The night's still young." He reached over and tugged gently on my left nipple, then looked into my face, tugged again and gave me a wet kiss on the lips.

"Kenny, what—"

"Don't say nothing, kid. It's okay." He grabbed my cock and began stroking it.

I had to know. All this touching—was it the beer or was Kenny into guys, too?

"Kenny," I began, breathing to the rhythm of his hand massaging my hard on, "what I've enjoyed most tonight is watching your ass. So whatever you have in mind now is okay with me."

I sat there shaking, stunned by what I'd just said.

The sound of the shower water stopped. Kenny's hand moved from my dick to the back of my neck. He pulled my face to his. Our tongues met. Then we heard the bathroom door knob jiggle and we quickly moved apart.

Mariana came into the room and said something in Spanish that made Kenny laugh. He told me Mariana thought I was pretty damn good for a first timer. They chatted in Spanish like old friends as Mariana moved around the room, getting ready to leave. Kenny went to his pants to get Mariana some cab money and helped her on with her coat. She gave us each a kiss before Kenny closed the door behind her. When she was gone, Kenny sat on the bed next to me and took my hand in his, stroking it gently.

"I dunno, kid, I feel funny about this."

"About what? Sticking your finger up my butt or kissing me?"

He laughed, then grew serious. "I'm not gonna bullshit you, kid, like, maybe I upset you by touching you. Anyway, you're a man now, far as I can tell. I guess you've fucked around enough to know what to expect from another guy."

"Wha-what do you mean?"

"We gotta be careful, a lot more careful than you've been at the Domino."

"What are you talking about?" I was dumbstruck. "Who told you? What'd they say?"

"Nothing much. One of the cooks saw you climbing into a truck on his way to work. You can't fool around in the neighborhood. Well, except for me maybe."

We laughed and he gave my cock a tug.

"Anyway, kid, you're a man now."

He gave my cock another tug and I got hard at his touch. He stroked my hard on and started kissing my neck. I reached behind him and massaged his ass cheeks. His lips nursed one of my nipples, then he licked his way up my face and we kissed for a long time, sucking tongue, trading spit, breathing heavily into one another's mouths. Finally he pulled back and looked at me with those sexy dark eyes.

"Kid, I want you to give my ass a real workout." He rolled over. "I saw how you got off fucking Mariana's hole. And a man's ass is tighter, hungrier. Only a man knows how good it makes another man's cock feel when he tightens his ass muscles around the hard-on sliding in and outta his ass. Put some of that Vaseline on your finger, kid, play with my hole a little."

I started to slowly probe his tight ass bud.

"Oh yeah, fucker," he gasped. "Feels so good. Stick your finger up my ass, kid ... oh shit, man, yeah." His ass let me in, then tightened around my digit. I fingered his hole deeper until my finger touched the soft and moist lining beyond his ass muscle. "Pull out and try it with two fingers."

Kenny had been right. His manly ass was tight and hungry. I fingered his butt and he sucked my dick. I was floating near orgasm when suddenly he pulled my cock out of his throat and said:

"I want to feel you inside me. I want to pull your cock up my ass and hear you begging for more." He tossed the jar of Vaseline my way. I caught it with my left hand, just like a pro. "Wipe some grease on your dick, make it easier on my hole."

Holding my dick with one hand, he faced away from me and slowly eased his hole onto my cockhead.

"Ok, kid, here goes ...watch my greedy ass swallow your cock ... Jeezus!"

I marveled at the sensation as his beautiful ass swallowed me whole.

"Just feel your cock, kid. Don't think about it, just ride the feeling. Don't think about nothing but how good your cock feels in my ass. Work on my tits, nice and gentle like."

I reached around, grabbed his swollen tits and twisted his nipples gently between my fingers.

"Feel your dick in my butt, kid. Float, baby."

"Kenny, I'm going to cum ... wait, oh, fuck."

He rode my cock harder.

"Kenny! Kenny!"

"Fuck, kid. Fuck. *Deme tu leche*. Shoot your fucking ball juice up my shitter. Jeezus, man, give it to me."

And then I lost it. I pulled his ass down on my cock and sprayed his guts with my spunk. Another pulse, and another, then my cock felt warm and wet, too wet, like maybe I'd peed.

Kenny rose up. I ran my fingers through the jizz and sweat on his ass. He held my hand there, then turned and gave me a lingering, wet kiss. When I opened my eyes, he was smiling.

"How about some dinner? Then we can get back to business."

"Kid, get up over me so I can suck your dick and play with your tits. I want to feel your cock get hard in my mouth. Come on."

"Kenny, I'm tired," I protested, turning away from him. We were back in the motel room, watching television after chowing down on fried chicken and French fries.

"Come on, kid, the night's young and so are you."

I crawled up over his chest, and inched my cock into his mouth. He reached up, massaged my tits and began twisting my sore nipples gently between his fingers. His right hand moved to my ass, and with his index finger, he traced the outline of my asshole.

"Just relax. Push down on my finger. That's it, sport." He continued to suck and stroke and probe, and once again I was in the mood.

"Turn around and sit on my face." Kenny grabbed my ass and swung me around. My face had nowhere to go but down on his purple-brown cockhead. I felt something warm and wet touch my asshole. Kenny was licking my ass, forcing his tongue ever deeper into my hole.

"Great ass, kid! I could lick this hole until tomorrow."

"Oh, Kenny," I moaned.

"This is just clearing the way for the real thing." He spread my ass cheeks and his tongue went in as far as it would go. "Just seeing how deep your hole is, kid."

My whole body began to tingle.

"Go with the feeling, fucker," he said.

My body pulsed to the steady rhythm set by his tongue. My hole felt warmer and wetter with every thrust. His whole mouth was up in my hole, licking, chewing, sucking, making the same wet noises as he made when he ate Mariana's pussy.

"Jeezus, this is just too good, kid."

I was close to cumming. I pulled Kenny's hand off my cock. Too late.

With every thrust of Kenny's tongue, I pumped another rope of ball juice onto his chest. Kenny's cock exploded in my throat. I couldn't swallow it fast enough. His cum drooled out of my mouth onto his cock and into his pubes.

"Jeezus, kid, I thought you'd never stop unloading!"

The next morning, I woke Kenny up by sucking his cock. "Damn, that feels good," he moaned. "Show me what you learned last night. Get Kenny's ass ready for your cock."

He lowered his ass on to my waiting tongue, then leaned over and slurped up my cock. I pried apart his ass cheeks and looked at his beautiful asshole, tracing the crack with my forefinger, playing with the puckered opening. I breathed in his sharp, clean, manly scent. The more I inhaled, the more I wanted him. Kenny sat upright and I fucked his ass with long, determined thrusts of my tongue. The base of my tongue started to hurt, but the pain, mingled with the exquisite man scent of Kenny's asshole, only heightened my excitement. He stroked my pulsing cock. I grabbed his, smeared his pre-cum over his bulging cock head and jerked him off.

His ass muscles tightened again around my tongue. His cock spurted jizz against on my stomach, cock and legs. As Kenny massaged his cum into my tits, I brought my cock to orgasm. Jizz shot out of my piss slit in every direction, hitting Kenny in the face and landing in his hair. I came so hard it hurt.

"There you go again, making a mess." He swung his body around so that we were face to face. "You know, kid, I think we might have something going for us here. We need to go camping more often."

We went "camping" quite a bit the rest of that wonderful summer. When the fall came and I went away to college in Santa Cruz, the emptiness I felt without Kenny's ass was never displaced by my new friends and my busy schedule. Oh, I had my share of new sexual adventures, but I eagerly anticipated each trip home and Kenny's monthly visits. We managed to get together a lot during my time as an undergrad, so I never went long without burying my face in his ass, feeling his warm mouth on my cock, or taking his dick up my own ass.

Shortly before graduation, I got a frantic call from Kenny, telling me he wouldn't be driving up with my folks for the ceremonies. His dad had suffered a stroke and he was going to spend some time with his parents. A few weeks later, we heard from Manny, the garage owner, that Kenny's dad had died. I must have called a dozen times over the next week, but the phone just rang and went unanswered.

Finally Kenny called, sounding tired, sad and confused. After we talked a while about his dad and the funeral, he cleared his throat, his voice straining.

"I'm not sure how to say this, kid, but just give me some space. I've got a lot going on right now."

"I have a chance to study overseas. I don't know what to do."

There was a pause; then, I could hear Kenny fumbling around. Probably looking for his pack of cigarettes.

"You gotta go, live your own life. I can't handle this thing with you right now."

"*Thing*?"

"I'm scared that if we keep going where we're going, we'll mess up both our lives."

"Kenny …"

"I'm sorry, kid, I don't know what to say. I'm just too tired to think. I'm not much of a letter writer, but let's try that for a while. We got a lot of stuff to talk about, kid, but now's not the time. There's just too much going on."

That summer I left to study and work in France. Kenny and I wrote back and forth for a while, then my letters went unanswered. Living in the city where my parents had met, married and lived brought new experiences into my life. I fell in love at least a half dozen times, but I never forgot Kenny.

Twelve years after graduating high school, I moved back to San Diego. One fall evening, as I walked into the Sheik lounge with my lover, Jack, I heard a raspier, deeper version of a familiar voice from a long lost time.

"Kid, is that you? Jeezus, ain't this something? Finally!" Kenny hopped down from a stool at the piano bar and gave me a bear hug so tight, I had to struggle to talk.

"My God, Kenny! You look great!" He was heavier now, with bright gray hair that framed his smooth mocha face. He looked at me with that quick, white smile and those mischievous eyes that I'd never forgotten. When he stepped back to take off his jacket, I could see from the tight fit of his pants that he still had the world's sexiest ass.

I introduced Kenny to Jack and Kenny introduced us to his partner Barry. Jack and Barry were both playful, sexy men who seemed to enjoy the sexual energy that passed between Kenny and me. The four of us talked, touched, laughed, groped and kissed. Then our lovers, both psychologists, started talking shop and became lost in their own conversation, which took them out on the patio.

"I love Barry and all," Kenny said after they were gone. "Couple of years after my dad passed, I was pretty miserable and drinking way too much. We hit it off and he turned me on to one of his associates for the therapy thing. Then we became lovers. Just couldn't keep his tongue outta old Kenny's butt."

"I know the feeling." I gave his ass a good squeeze.

"I had a lot going on in my head back then, like figuring out if I was straight or gay or whatever. Much as I like guys, you ain't going to see me marching in no parade. And I still like banging a hot broad now and then. But the relationship thing is a lot easier with another guy these days." Kenny drew closer. "You know, kid, I still can't believe it, us running into each other like this."

"Let's get some air," I said, feeling overwhelmed. We went

out to the patio, past Jack and Barry, who were deep in conversation.

"Sorry about dropping out of your life the way I did." Kenny leaned against the patio bar. "There was just too much going on, my dad being sick and all. His dying got me thinking about my own life. I was falling for you and I was scared. There wasn't a day that I didn't think about you, hoping that maybe you found more in life than you would have with old Kenny."

I grabbed his hand. "I loved you and I was happy. There really isn't more in life than that. I've had a wonderful life, but you were the start of that life for me."

"So I did something for you back then? I did more than make your cock and ass feel good?"

"You made a difference in my life, a good difference."

He started crying on my shoulder, then stepped back, embarrassed, and lit a cigarette. I pulled it from his lips, took his handsome face in my hands and drew his mouth to mine. We kissed, his mustache pressed into mine, his tongue exploring my mouth. The same feeling that overwhelmed me the first night I tasted Kenny's ass—the feeling that had bound me to him all those years ago—thundered through my being. Once more, my hands grasped the fullness of his still-hard ass. Then he pulled back just enough to catch my eyes in his gaze.

"Why don't we see if it does a number on you the way it used to?"

I never could say no to Kenny's ass.

Rimworld

RANDY BOYD

*C*lick.

"And now, the KAZZ Saturday Night Movie. Tonight: Ben Sniffer and Matt Dildo are in love with the same beautiful, manly butthole and will do anything to get a taste of it. It's the outrageous, madcap comedy, *There's Something About Ass.*"

Click.

"ButtMusicTelevision is proud to bring you a world premiere video, the newly remixed single from rock legends KISS: 'I Was Made for Licking You, Baby, and You Were Made for Licking Me.'"

Click.

"Tonight on *69/69*, a special report: Parasites: Enemy of Us All. What are they? Where are they? And what you can do to avoid the scourge of rimmers everywhere. Plus, a *69/69* exclusive, a live, in-depth Booty Walters interview with the leader of the Amoebas."

Booty Walters: "Is it your goal to disrupt the joy of eating ass for every single buttman on the planet?"

Amoeba Bin Laden: "Big juicy buttocks be the work of the devil. Satan! Satan!"

Booty Walters: "Can you tell us why?"

Announcer: "A *69/69* you can't afford to miss. Tonight."

Click.

"And now for our *SportsButtCenter* Showcase Game of the Night, the Denver Broncos at the Minnesota Vikings. This was a hotly contested match-up that featured 6'4", 260 pound Viking QB Daunte Culpepper bending over a record 58 times in the first half, exposing his massive, high and tight muscle butt in more ways than a power bottom in a porno flick—albeit the black gladiator Culpepper's ass was covered by Minnesota's sheer white football pants, unlike a porn bottom's butt which is covered by nothing but gallons of Elbow Grease and cum. But we digress. Sir Daunte's beefy booty put on quite a show tonight, bending, stretching, running, lunging and, at one point, squatting to cover a Chris Kilgore fumble—*muchas gracias*, Mr. Kilgore."

Kilgore (naked, sweaty, sitting on the can in the locker room): "The ball was stripped from my hands and I just thank God that Daunte's huge black ass was big enough to squat down on it and smother it between those massive butt cheeks to prevent the defense from recovering the ball."

Announcer: "But Bronco butts did not just sit idly by and let Minnesota rub their noses in it. Denver countered with all-pro running back Terrell Davis's bootilicious back. Terrell, who gave the camera 28 butt shots in the first quarter alone, might wanna consider a new nickname: chocolate, *chocolate* thunderbooty. Coming back from a career-threatening groin injury just three weeks ago ... ouch ... Davis's 210 pound, compact ebony rump romped up and down the Metrodome turf as if his ass was twitching, itching and in need of a very long tongue. Any volunteers? As you can tell by this shot of Terrell bending over to tie his shoelaces in the fourth quarter, those not into hot sweaty crack need not apply. Davis and Culpepper's big black booties battled for the spotlight all night long, but in the end—pun intended—Daunte was victorious, showing us his ass a whopping 19 more times than Davis. Oh, a footnote to our *SportsButtCenter* Showcase game: the Vikes won the actual football game, 31-17."

Click.

"Straight from the '90s, here's the boy band All-4-Ass with the ButtMusicTelevision Hall of Fame video: 'I Can Lick You Like That.'"

Click.

"Listen, mon, ass be Irie as we say in my Jamaica, but just because a butt look good in jeans don't mean it'll taste good out of jeans. Ya hear me? Call me now! $3.99 a minute. The Booteemon tell you all ya need ta know. The hole truth. Dat's the H-O-L-E truth. Get it? Call me now!"

Click.

"Now you all know how the game is played. When the bell sounds, each contestant will race through those studio doors and out into the streets of Chicago. The first contestant to lick the

asses of ten consenting male strangers will win $50,000 and
return tomorrow as defending champion for a chance at another 50 grand. Our two runners-up today will get $100 per ass they
rim. Now ... remember, if you approach a group of men that
know each other, you can *only* lick one of their asses—well, you
can lick more of them if you like, but *only one* of those asses will
count toward the magic number of ten. Are our three contes-
tants ready? Camera crews ready? Studio audience ready? It's
time to play *Been There, Licked That!*"

    Click.

    "And the number one requested video again this week on
Butt Entertainment Television, for the 15th straight week—
don't even bother with the drum roll—it's Whipme Houston
and a hint of reggae in da house with 'Your Ass in My Face and
My Ass in Your Face.'"

    Click.

    "Welcome back to the Butt News Network's weekend edi-
tion of *Crackfire*, where we debate the issues as they happen.
Today is all about which is the better eye candy: football butts or
baseball butts. Now, before the break, Senator Olefart, you were
saying we also need to be looking at WWF butt."

    "I tell you this, ole sonny boy, them world wide wrestling
derrières ought to come with a warning label similar to the ones
we put on plastic bags: caution, you could smother yourself
when burying your face deep inside these massive mountains of
ass."

    Click.

    "This Saturday, get ready for a world television premiere
event. It's the 1950s like you've never seen 'em when four horny

sailors with big, beautiful, beefy bubble butts land in the middle
of Spring Break in Cancun for some fun, sun and some really
long tongues. Don't miss the outrageous premiere of *Where the
Butts Are*, coming Saturday."

Click.

The Sony remote sank deeper into the sofa cushion,
becoming one with Howard's musky butt crack, which was covered by Howard's smelly blue workmen's khakis. Typical night in
the small box of a house: empty beer mug next to two polished-
off TV dinners on the coffee table, hound dog sound asleep on
his back like a dead bug, and Howard, sawing logs on the couch
'til round three in the morning, when he'd drag his huge
plumber's ass to the bedroom for a few more z's before the sun
came up.

Nice life. Nice routine. Neither the long black Sony remote
nor the plumber's massive round beach ball of a butt could ask
for anything more.

Click.

Getting a Taste

MARC EADMON

It started out like any other evening: first some TV—*Buffy: The Vampire Slayer, Angel,* the news—then we headed for Gary's bedroom.

"Give me one of your massages?" he asked.

"Sure, *papi,* you know I love pampering you. Get undressed while I get the oil."

When I came back to the bedroom, Gary was on the bed, his caramel-colored booty reaching toward the ceiling.

Lawd ha' mercy!

Gary worked really hard to develop what nature had given him—and it showed. He was 6'1" with broad shoulders, a small, tapered waist and serious black man booty. His face was clean-shaven and smooth—except for a tiny scar near his right ear—and his brown eyes slanted slightly, as if, somewhere down the line, he had Asian in his family. From the top of his fade to the soles of his shoes, all 220 pounds of him were a walking work of art.

"You gonna keep looking at my ass all night?" he asked.

"For your information, I was looking at your everything. You're a beautiful man and I'm blessed to be with you." I undressed down to my underwear and sat down on the bed. He twisted around and gave me a kiss.

"That makes two of us, baby." He planted another kiss and lay back down. "Now can I get my massage?"

"Yes, sir. Right away, sir!" I poured some oil into the palm of my hand.

"Thank you, baby. I really do appreciate it. I'm a little sore from the workout."

"I told you to stop after that fourth set, but nooooo! You had to be Superman."

My Superman.

In his early 30s like me, Gary was everything I wanted in a mate. He was intelligent, funny and generous and had no problem letting me know how he felt about me. He had a masculine air about him that moved me, as did the way he spoke, laughed and walked. His physical appearance aside, we were both spiritual and I felt comfortable being open with him about my feelings, which had grown exponentially in the last few months.

Oh, and the sex! Damn, that man knew how to handle his. *Ya heard me?* I definitely did not have a problem with his being the top in our relationship. Hell, I was almost getting used to him calling me his "dark chocolate shorty." (I mean, I *was* 5'7", 160 wet.)

"Where's it hurt?" I asked him. He reached around and placed my hand on his lower back.

"Right there. Oooo, baby, that feels good!"

After a while, my hands neared his beautiful butt, but Gary clenched his cheeks nervously.

"Why you squeezing your ass together, baby?" I asked. "What you think I'm gonna do? Relax, I know the rules."

"I ain't uptight."

"Haven't I been good, concentrating on just your back?"

"You managed to cop a couple of feels."

Guilty as charged. Yes, I wanted to dive in face first into his perfectly sculpted caramel mounds, but Gary had made something quite clear the day we met almost a year ago.

We were slow dancing at a friend's party, he had just cupped my ass and I was about to return the favor. "Don't mess with my ass," he had said. "Don't even think about it. I'm a top dawg."

"Oh," I had said, pulling back from him a little. "You're one of those guys who feels he's too much of a man to get fucked, huh?"

"Come on, shorty, you're tripping. It ain't like that. I tried it and didn't like it. I hope that's not gonna be a problem."

"Just as long as you understand that I have a dick and I like ass, too. Now if I can't get in it, I at least have to be able to feel on it and get my face up in it!"

We'd been working on the issue ever since. He didn't protest as much anymore, but he still didn't let me toss his salad. In the few months since we'd been a couple, I had tried a sneak attack a couple of times, but he always busted me before I got a taste.

Now, as he lay on the bed, I began massaging his thighs,

working my way down his calves, then back up. Unable to restrain myself any longer, I placed a hand on each cheek and began to massage.

"Relax," I said before he could object. "Glutes are muscles, too!"

I only stayed there for a minute. I wanted him to know that I wouldn't try anything he wouldn't like. I had him turn over so I could finish his full body massage. When I got to his chest, I straddled his waist, careful not to place my ass directly on his manhood. I didn't want him getting too excited—yet. Gary, however, had other plans. He placed his hands around my waist, set me down right on top of his crotch, then began a circular grind while pulling at the elastic band in my underwear.

"Okay, *papi*, I see you want the Total Release Massage." I rolled over to one side and finished removing my underwear. Straddling him once again, I leaned down to kiss him. Our tongues played with each other as we grinded our hips together. Gary had his hands in their favorite position: on my ass, kneading it much the same way I had tried to knead his earlier.

"Oh, baby, I want to make love to you so bad," Gary moaned.

"I know you do, *papi*, but first I gotta get a taste of that dick." I slid down his body, kissing and nibbling along the way. I stopped to suck on both nipples, then lick his underarms. By the time I reached his groin, he was writhing. I licked up the length of his shaft until I reached the head, where I made circles with my tongue.

"Stop teasing me, baby, suck it!"

I looked up at him and said: "Feed it to me, daddy."

He made his dick jump and I took him in my mouth. Eight and a half inches of Grade-A, choice tube steak. I tried getting as much of it as I could down my throat using one hand to assist, but Gary caught me, as always: "Move your hand."

Papi wanted to feel only lips and tongue on his root. Not a problem. I've got mad skills when it comes to playing the skin flute, but I'm not a deep throat expert. Gary suddenly thrust upwards. I gagged and had to pull back a bit. I tried again and got more of him down my throat. I could feel his pulse beating as I used my tongue to trace one of the veins running along his dick.

"Oh shit, baby, swing that ass up here so I can taste that hole."

I swiveled around until my ass was over his face. He flicked his tongue around my asshole, teasing me until I begged him: "Yes baby, eat that ass!" I serviced his tool more passionately to egg him on. I sucked on his balls, and then … my tongue had a mind of its own. I started licking his ass …

"Oooo damn, baby."

Just the reaction I was hoping for. I decided to go for broke and actually stuck my tongue in his asshole.

"Awww, fuck, baby, that feels good! Do that shit!"

I couldn't swing around fast enough. I had been waiting for this moment for four months! I got between his legs and started eating away. Gary wrapped his legs around me, as if to keep me where I was.

Like I was planning on going anywhere!

I tried to push his legs up so I could get at that hole better, but Gary had a better idea. He swung one leg over my head until he was on his stomach. (I don't think he felt comfortable having his legs up in the air.) Regardless, it afforded me easier access and I could still look at, smell and feel his ass all at the same time. I was in ass eater's heaven! Gary doesn't have a lot of body hair, so his ass is smooth like butta, baby!

I pulled him back until he was on his knees and stuck my tongue in as far as it would go. I felt his sphincter contract and could have cum right then. My dick was rock hard and dripping pre-cum. I reached around to stroke Gary's dick. It was equally hard.

"Yes, baby," Gary growled. "Stroke that dick for me!"

I played with his piece, alternating my tongue between his balls and his asshole. Both of us were breathing hard and starting to sweat. The next thing I knew, Gary pulled away and turned onto his back again.

"Whew! Okay, baby, that's enough of that."

"Says who?"

Gary pulled me up so that we were face to face again. "I just wanted to try something new and I know you wanted it, too."

We kissed, a deep soul kiss.

"Thank you," I said. "I've wanted to do that for the longest. And now for something I know you want to do." I straddled him again and reached over to the night-stand to grab some lube and a condom. I opened the package with my teeth, then placed the condom on his penis with my mouth.

"Should I ask where you learned that?"

I laughed and winked up at him. "That safe-sex workshop a few months ago. Did you like it?"

"Hell yeah! That ass ready for me, baby? I want to be inside you." He grabbed his dick and began stroking it. I poured some lubricant in my hand, oiled him up and straddled him again. He worked his slick finger into my asshole, then another.

"Yeah, *papi*, open that ass up!" I reached back and placed the head of his dick against my hole, then let his cock work its way in. I kept going until I felt his pubic hair against my ass. "Aww fuck!" Even though we had been fucking on the regular for a while now, that initial entry still hurt a bit. Gary was not a small man.

"You okay, baby?"

I started to ride him.

"I'll take that as a yes. Damn, that ass feels good!" He thrust upwards, meeting me as I came down. "This my ass, baby?" He flipped us over so that I was on my back and placed my feet against his chest.

Brothaman started laying some serious pipe!

"Don't you ever give this ass to anybody else!" he grunted.

"Never, nigga. It's all yours." I grabbed his ass, pulled him even deeper and massaged his dick with my sphincter muscles. From my vantage point, I could see the two of us in the mirror on Gary's closet. Mostly I could see Gary's powerful back, leading down to that impossibly small waist, power booty and muscular thighs. He looked over his shoulder and saw what I was looking at.

"Oh! So you want to watch me get up in that ass, huh?" Without waiting for a response, he scooped me up and changed our position so we were lying across the bed. This way we could see both of us a lot clearer. "*Aiight* then, let me really give you something to watch!"

He wrapped his hands around my thighs and pulled me toward him till he had his feet on the floor and my ass was at the edge of the bed. I knew I was in for a serious dick-down now.

"You ready baby?" he asked, teasing me with slow, long strokes.

"Yes, *papi*, give it to me."

Gary started fucking me like I said something bad about his mama. At one point, he flipped me over so I was on my knees.

"I wanna look at that pretty ass while I'm getting up in it. Yeah baby, give …that … ass … up!"

My man was not playing! The sounds of our bodies slapping together mixed with the sounds of our moans. I was getting close to cumming. I told Gary. He put me on my back, took one of my ankles in each hand and really began to pile-drive my ass while I jacked my dick.

"Yeah, come on, baby, cum for daddy!"

"Oh shit, baby. Here it comes!"

The first shot landed on my neck. That's all Gary needed to see to get his nut, too.

"Goddamn, this ass is good!"

He was so loud, I knew the neighbors were getting an earful!

"You're making me cum! Awwww fuuuuuuuk!" I could feel him throbbing inside me as he released his load. Still in the midst of my own orgasm, I yelled:

"Yeah *papi*, that's *what* I wanted! Oh man! I love you!"

Afterwards, after we came to our senses, Gary smiled at me and said, "Damn, baby, you been holding that one for a while?"

"Part of it was the excitement of eating your ass," I said.

He blushed like a schoolboy. "Well, I didn't really like it."

I took the cum towel he gave me to clean myself up, knowing I had to handle this situation delicately. For a brotha like him not used to having someone rim him, it was probably difficult to admit he liked it.

"You a I-didn't-like-it lie," I busted out laughing. "The way you were pushing your ass in my face, I thought I was gonna suffocate."

The shocked look on his face was priceless.

"I'm just picking on you baby!"

He gave me a petulant look, and for a second, I saw the little boy he once was. He tried to pull away from me, but I wrapped my legs around him and pulled him down on top of me. "Come on now, don't be like that. You and I both know that you were frontin', right?"

He let out a deep sigh, but at least he stopped struggling.

"Right?" I insisted.

He nodded his head in response.

"*Aiight*," I said. "Now, I know you're not gonna all of a sudden be this big bottom boy and I'm cool with the way things are. But if you ever feel like you want some dick, let me know."

He tried his hardest not to laugh, but couldn't hold it.

"Okay, okay, you got me," he said. "But I got something on you, too!"

"That being?"

"Did you mean it when you said you love me?"

Now it was my turn to blush. I hid my face in his shoulder. I hadn't meant to say it aloud, but I did mean it. I raised my head and looked him in the eye. "Yeah, I mean it. I love you."

We lay there looking into each other's eyes until he said, "Good, 'cause I love you too."

We had finally said what had been unspoken for the longest time. He leaned down and kissed me, then said, "Now, let's take a shower and get all this sex washed off."

That was a couple of weeks ago. Since then Gary and I have been looking for a place we can call ours. We both agree that it's important for a couple to start off living together in a neutral space. Tonight though, we're at my place. I'm in the bedroom and Gary just got out of the shower. We're meeting some friends for dinner later tonight.

"Baby?" Gary says from the bathroom. "Would you mind putting some oil on my back?"

"Sure *papi*." I watch him as he walks into the bedroom butt naked and glistening from the shower. He stops in the doorway, gives me this sexy look and says, "Maybe we can also do that thing I don't like." He lies across the bed booty up, looking at me seductively.

Aretha said it best: "When my baby calls, I jump to it."

Appreciating My Assets

JAY STARRE

I do a lot of squats. The goal, of course, is a nice solid ass. If it's a touch on the large side, that doesn't bother me, as long as it's muscular. All my strenuous labour has produced results, too. When I look in the mirror on the wall in my bedroom, I am more than a little pleased. With another mirror propped on the bed, I can scrutinize my own butt, and it is truly awesome.

I appreciate what I see: my assets, so to speak. I love my own butt, to tell the honest truth. I love the way it's round and yet muscular and I love the way it feels: smooth, shaved, firm and taut. I love the enjoyment I get spreading it wide and taking a cock or fingers or whatever up it, getting reamed and rammed and satisfied in every anal way I can.

I am so appreciative of the results of my efforts in the gym,

I often spend time in front of the mirror in my bedroom giving my butt a good sexual workout. I usually start by stripping off my clothes, getting nice and naked, and propping the mirror up on the bed so I can easily observe my butt from all angles. I take a long appreciative look at it, running my hands over it, feeling the curved mounds, pulling them apart and getting a look at the deep crack and the pouting butt hole in the centre. I run my fingers up my anal crevice, groping for the hole, sliding fingertips over the palpitating slot, sighing with intense pleasure. I shave my butt—the cheeks, the crack and hole itself. I love the appearance of big muscular glutes, all hairless, with no blemishes whatsoever. Although I can get a good tan, I have a fairly white butt. I'm Irish and have pale skin "where the sun don't shine." My ivory-white butt stands out like a sexual beacon, calling all those interested in a look, a feel or a fuck.

When I'm alone, it's up to me to give my delectable butt a good working over. I feel it for a while, teasing the crack and hole lightly. With tantalizing finger strokes, I drive myself into a heightened state of excitement and anticipation. Then I get out the lube and the dildos. I usually start with a small one, something that will open me up but not force my sensitive hole to expand too rapidly. I have a dildo that's very realistic with a tapered head, no balls and a flat bottom. I put one leg on the bed and spread my cheeks, bending over and watching in the mirror as I slide the lubed dildo all over my crack, revelling in the sight of the glistening grease as it coats my hard butt cheeks and hairless crevice. The dildo slides over my butt hole, tickling my sensitive ass rim. I shudder at the touch, thinking about how it will feel when that hard rubber begins to enter, stretching me open and filling my guts.

I settle down on the hole, pointing the head of the dildo at the entrance, and tease myself with light pokes. I sigh, then grunt as a bit of the tapered head slips past the taut ass ring. I watch, mesmerized as my hand holds the dildo right on target and begins to shove it inside me. I'm moaning by the time I push the entire head past my butt rim into the tunnel beyond. My thighs are shaking and my cock is rock-hard, slapping against my belly. I stroke my meat a few times to arouse myself even more but then leave it, concentrating on the delicious sensation of fat, hard rubber sliding into my aching guts.

Inch by inch, I bury the dildo inside me, then pull it out slowly, gazing hungrily at my butt hole as it opens up and expands around the hard rubber girth. The ass lips pucker out as the dildo slides out, then slides back in. I pump my butt hole with the fake cock, in and out, deep and shallow, grunting like a pig. There is a little trick I employ with this particular dildo. Once I get my asshole really lubed up—by adding another handful of slippery goo to the shaft of the dildo and around my gaping hole—I begin to press the entire length of it deeper and deeper until it hangs right at the end, barely showing. I let go of it and stare in the mirror at my big hard ass and that round end of the dildo just barely poking out. What a sight. Then I go farther. I use one fingertip and slowly prod the end of the dildo deeper, deeper until it disappears, the puckered rim of my butt hole snapping shut around it.

I feel the thing way up my guts, filling me, stretching me, poking at my prostate. But nothing shows in the mirror, just my greasy white ass, taut and quivering. I squirm around the buried dildo, then spread my legs, squat down and let it slide back out, all the way. It feels unreal.

After that's gotten me all hot and bothered, I usually get out the butt plug, a big fat thing that starts out with a tapered point and gets fatter and fatter before it narrows again and terminates in a big square base. I squat and point it at my parted ass cheeks, staring at myself in the mirror, at the way my powerful butt muscles spread out from my waist when I squat, at the slippery, greased ass crack wide open and butt plug slowly disappearing up my hole. Its size grows larger and larger, my poor butt hole expanding desperately to accept the humongous girth of it. I grunt and strain. I finally get down on my knees and bend over. The largest part of the butt plug stretches me wide, my asshole gaping red and greasy as the rubber expands me. The plug suddenly becomes narrower, pulling itself deeper by the abrupt contraction of my ass rim, those quivering contractions pulling the plug all the way inside until only the square flange is visible.

I am stuffed. My ass aches wonderfully. I let go of the butt plug, my ass rim snug around it. Then I begin to whack off. I beat my hard meat mercilessly, pounding my pud and staring at my beautiful butt-plugged ass in the mirror. My greasy mounds writhe and quiver. I squirm around the plug, crawling on my hands and knees as one hand moves rapidly up and down my greased cock. I get on my back and raise my thighs, staring at my wide-spread butt in the mirror, watching the square flange of the plug snap in and out as I come closer and closer to complete satisfaction.

I finally shoot my wad, cum rocketing out of my burning dick head. I squeeze out the plug at the same instant, shouting out my satisfaction as it plops to the rug and my violated asshole gapes empty, drooling lube. I lie on the floor and whimper.

That's a good jerk off session for me, but even better is a good workout from a stud who also appreciates hot butt. For that, I go to the bathhouse. I love to get a room and dim the lights. I want the guy who is checking me out to be forced to peer inside, getting closer until he finds himself being seduced by the miracle of my awesome butt.

I kneel on the bed, my ass facing the door. I also get a room with a mirror by the bed so I can watch myself getting plugged. My favourite trick is to bring a dildo, and one in particular really turns me on. It's called the Assmaster. It's a good two feet long and has a convenient handle on one end. A person can hold the Assmaster by the handle and shove it in and out of a willing butt hole, the round knob at the tip eliciting delightful sensations as it bombards the innards of the person getting ploughed.

I lay the Assmaster on the bed between my spread thighs, an obscenely sexy object to entice my prey into my lair. Of course, my big hot ass should be enough to bring a true butt lover in. It's shaved and greased and primed for action. I stare at the door and wait, my legs spread.

When someone acceptable arrives to peer inside, his eyes grow wide as he takes in the sight of me naked on my knees, my hot ass parted and available, I stare into his eyes and will him to enter. When he spots the Assmaster, he has no choice but to groan and slip into the room, shutting the door behind him. He discards his towel. He is good looking or I don't let him in; but he has to be a bit on the raunchy side, eager to shove that gross object way up my guts and provide me with the hard fucking I crave.

I spread my thighs wider and thrust my ass toward him, an

unsubtle invitation to sample the wares. My hole glistens with lube, twitching with the excitement. My good-looking stud's mouth is open with appreciative lust as he reaches to touch me with shaky fingers. I close my eyes and sigh as I feel the first tentative caresses, fingers running over my butt cheeks, down from my waist, then around the lower portion of hard butt mound, then inexorably into the parted crevice, sliding toward the goal, the prize, my quaking, trembling butt hole.

"What an awesome ass!" he sighs as two of his fingers settle on my greasy slot and begin to slide into it.

"It's all yours, buddy." I thrust my hungry butt backward into his hands.

"What do you like?" His voice quivers as he strokes in and out with two fingers. That feels fucking great, those digits frigging me lightly, opening me up. He breathes heavily and stares in awe at my fantastic ass, which is wide open and waiting for him. I can tell by the look in his eyes that he can hardly believe his good fortune.

"I want you to work that big Assmaster up my guts, fill me with it, then fuck my butt good with it." I look into his eyes in the mirror.

"Whatever you say," he murmurs, looking down at the huge dildo between us on the bed. He is quick to lift it up with his free hand, wrapping his fist around the handle. The other end flops around, the bulbous head looking brutal.

"Go ahead. I want it." I wiggle my butt around his buried fingers which have slithered as deep as they could go. He removes the fingers and places the bulb at the entrance, fascinated by the image, his blue eyes round and focused. He shoves.

It slides right inside me, the ball disappearing at once. I groan. He shoves deeper, then deeper again.

"Go ahead, work the whole big thing in there."

"Can you take it?" He slides more of the dildo inside me, in awe of the fact that a good seven inches have disappeared into my seemingly bottomless butt pit.

"Shove it all the way in!" My thighs are shaking, my asshole is on fire.

He goes for it. With one fist on the handle and the other holding my ass cheeks apart, he fills me to the limit with the Assmaster. My prostate is mashed; my guts are on fire. He keeps on shoving. I let out a huge breath and relax totally.

"It's in!" he says in disbelief. "It's all the fucking way in!"

"Fuck me with it!" I open my eyes and watch in the mirror beside us. My muscular ass clenches and flexes with each powerful thrust of the Assmaster. The head mashes my prostate and teases my guts. My cock grows stiffer. I will explode if he keeps it up.

"You like that?" He grunts as he pummels me. "Do you like this Assmaster pounding your beautiful big ass?"

"I fucking love it!"

He shoves harder and I begin to shoot.

"You're drilling the cum right out of me!"

I press my face into the bed, spewing all over the sheets. He keeps pounding while his own cum rains down on my writhing butt.

He abandons me, the dildo sticking out of my violated butt hole. I sprawl on the bed, overcome with the power of my orgasm. I am totally satiated. Until I wiggle my big hard ass and feel the Assmaster still inside me. Then I know I want more. I want it again. And again.

The night is young, my assets still intact. Maybe someone else will be appreciative.

I think so.

Comfort Station

BILLY TWEE

Fashions change, and thank God for that. For far too long, the men's fashion gods have told us to wear trousers that hang full and loose. It's quite a change from the days of my youth, when tight was right. Tight pants were hot in leather, of course, but they were almost as good in plain old cotton, as long as they were cut to outline the thigh, belly and butt, and oh, so indiscreetly, what you packed up front. The seam at the crotch was cut so high and tight, your cock had to be dressed left or right, whichever you fancied, and your balls were squeezed and set in place to reveal however much you dared.

Sometimes I fear those days must be gone forever, because lately, fashion designers have been putting us into pants that are lots worse than merely baggy, lots worse. Call them aggressively asexual, cut so that all the attributes of male potency must be

left to the imagination. I hate what the stores are selling nowa-
days. Not satisfied with emasculating the male form with artless
Dockers, they've advanced their assault on male sexuality with
peg-legged chinos straight out of the dorky '50s.

But I'm getting off point. I am a butt lover. I love to touch
'em, sniff 'em, lick 'em, eat 'em and drill 'em. And I'm hardly
ever satisfied by merely contemplatin' 'em. I'd rather see 'em—
not just think about 'em. That's why my lunch hours in San
Francisco are so important. I can fantasize about male butt any
ole time, but during my lunch hour, I can hit the street and sniff
'em out. Especially during those rare hot days. Those T-shirt and
jeans days. Those tank and cutoff days. I'm out there—at the
Bank of America world headquarters, or the Yerba Buena Center
in the Crocker Galleria, or the plaza at Montgomery and Market
in the City's financial heart— just waiting to catch the guy who
bucks fashion trends and likes to wear *his* high and tight.

During my sightseeing, I dismiss all dudes in baggy pants
right from the start: the sweaty bike messengers, the hip students
hurrying to the Academy of Art, the cloaked Financial District
types. Not to mention the tourists from here, there and wherev-
er. They may all have fine butts, if you could *find* their butts,
which thanks to The Gap and its imitators, are usually lost within folds of fabric. There are some guys who still wear their pants
tight, though. It's just too bad they're in their forties now and
must rein their middle-aged asses into jeans euphemistically
referred to as "full cut." No, thanks.

So when I see a younger dude in a nice set of tight trousers,
my faith in this supremely male world is restored. I rejoice in my
conviction that fashions can and do change, if only more men

would stop listening to The Gap and forge their own trails toward masculine affirmation.

Like this dude coming my way just now. It's lunch hour in Union Square, kinda warmish by San Francisco standards. He's Latin, I'm guessing, maybe Mediterranean with dark skin and black hair coaxed into trendy spikes by a generous application of gel. He's got an aura of casual sex around him, transmitting the message that anything's possible if it's warm and moves. He's about five-eight but nicely packed into a turquoise tank top, black flared trousers and black leather platform slides without socks.

Can it get any better? How about that flat stomach? And those defined arms, slightly tensed? The trousers are cut high to the waist, closely following the contour of his ass, hugging his cheeks firmly and keeping those buns aloft and high flying, as if defying gravity.

I'm sitting in a plastic chair on the sidewalk by Sammy's Deli on Sutter Street as this number approaches, making his way past the Banana Republic store where he's obviously not shopped. He's wearing a black leather pouch attached to a thin strap that crosses his chest and fits neatly just under his armpit. A pouch containing ...? The bare necessities, I hope: cab fare and a condom.

He walks past me with a swaggering gait, no doubt due in part to his shoes, which are designed more for styling than walking. Seconds later, he's down the block, giving me a full rear view of his magnificent ass in those tight black trousers. The contour of his small, nicely curved buns is more than enticing. A barely visible seam in his pants splits the butt crack, dividing then cupping each bun bewitchingly. Sweet Jesus, I'll never be able to get the image out of my mind.

Did I say Latin? I'm quite sure of it now. Those Native American genes are surely responsible for the tight, firm, little buttocks, so wonderful to contemplate and even nicer to touch, I'm sure.

He's noticed my interest and looks back as he reaches the corner. I look straight at him, not concerned about concealing my enthusiasm. He turns to the right and disappears behind the record shop on the corner.

Well, let's not be shy.

I get up and hurry to the intersection. He's halfway down the block but in no particular hurry, so it's not hard to catch up. He's hard to lose as his turquoise top stands out like a beacon among the sea of neutrals, blacks, grays. He waits for the light to change and then crosses Post, continuing on his way toward Market Street.

What's his story? I wonder. He can't be a hustler. They're into baggy jeans like everyone else. He as sure as hell ain't no cop.

Carry on. This pursuit must be resolved.

He crosses Market Street and pauses by one of the city's public comfort stations. For those of you unfamiliar with this phenomenon, I'll be brief. It took a French company to think them up: a public self-cleaning rest room contained in a steel bullet-shaped housing, always painted dark green and situated strategically along the city's most popular thoroughfares. There's something kind of *fin-de-siècle* about them, picturesque and anachronistic (American know-how hasn't come up with anything better). I've never had the chance to take advantage of these conveniences, but that's about to change. My Latin man-bait enters the comfort station on Market Street as if he owns it. Moments later, I make my move and follow him in, without regard for anyone who might notice two men going into one solo restroom.

My man is most definitely Latin, with big, gorgeous dark eyes and a five o'clock shadow. The shadow (cultivated, I'm sure) evokes an arresting blue collar roughness, an effect tempered only slightly by a gold stud in the left ear. He raises his muscled arms over his head and presses them against the wall, looking back at me over his shoulder as he allows his trousers to fall to the ground.

I drop to my knees and bury my face in the crevice of his ripe, brown ass. I grab his butt cheeks and spread them wide, allowing myself to plunge forward, deep into his valley of ass sweat, redolent with the scent of rich, humid, mossy peat. My tongue probes deeper until I find his quivering puckerhole, fresh with manscent, moist and ripe. He rifles through his pouch and opens up a small plastic tube of hair gel, then places the tube firmly into my own hand. Next he guides my hand until the tube is placed squarely on the ring of his pinkish-brown asshole. I squeeze the tube, emitting a clear and thick, viscous goo. I don't stop until all of its contents are emptied into the receptacle at the deep end of his shitter. For a few lovely moments, he tenses the muscles of his ass cheeks causing shallow depressions to form in the flesh while the inner channels of his butt hole churn the sticky pudding deep within. This demonstration of muscular control is accompanied by delicious farting sounds straight from the sloppiest of holes.

My man spreads his thighs ever farther apart and raises his ass ever so slightly to accommodate my head as my tongue licks all around his juicy butt hole. I lap all the gel that has strayed onto his coffee-colored ass before returning to his manhole, now oozing a bead of gel. Grunting, my man goes to work, pushing out pearl after pearl of gel from his asshole with perfectly measured control. I lapped each glistening pearl and playfully let it dance on the tip of my tongue before retracting and spreading the gel throughout the caverns of my mouth. The sticky butt-sauce has an earthy, peaty flavor that recalls raw sex in Buena Vista Park after midnight, or at construction sites on sweaty days during summer, or in the bushes halfway to the summit of Mt. Tam.

My man looks at me over his shoulder, watching me devour every drop of jelly agitated by his ass muscles. With complete and final abandon, I lick the remains of the sticky gel clustered around his pulsing sphincter and swallow it all, feeling its voyage all the way down to the deep vaults of my gut.

My Latin man hoists his pants up to his navel. From where I sit on the floor, I see his perfectly sculpted buttocks above me, split by the seam of his pants into two gorgeous balls of flesh. And then he is gone. Without a word.

No matter, I'll see you again, you little bugger, and we'll do this again. Bet your ass.

And now I read in various magazines and newspapers—it's not important which ones—that other American cities are considering the purchase of French comfort stations. Let me weigh in on this subject: do it and do it now. Your taxpayers' dollars couldn't be better spent. Everyone's entitled to a little comfort. Just think of the possibilities.

In Praise of Big Black Ass

MATTHEW STEWARD

We all have our preferences. And when it comes to ass-lovers, we are all wholly dedicated to our particular favorites. Some prefer small, tight and smooth, others wide, fleshy and hairy. There are, of course, an infinite variety in between. For me, nothing beats a big, bubble butt. And the *crème de la crème* is the well-built black man with plenty of ass to go around. While the bubble butt is not solely the domain of black folks, you'll find many more big butts on blacks than on whites. For whatever the reason, I'm grateful. It's what makes walking the streets of New York or watching certain sports all the more enjoyable.

At gay bars, many of us stand against the wall so we can all check each other out. Obviously, this precludes being able to check out the ass, but alas, there are other pleasures beyond the butt, like spotting a man with a beautiful smile. On one such occasion I gazed across the bar at a beefy, medium-toned man with a gorgeous smile. We played the cruising game for a while until I drew near and said hello. He was even better up close. He was very nicely built—not cut, but meaty with a little give to his muscle. That is probably my favorite type of body—strong and muscular, but a bit thick.

My preference for this kind of body is in no small part due to the ass that usually comes with it, especially on the broths: a nice, big, round, muscular butt with some added meat that significantly enhances the allure. While I'm also a fan of the ripped glutes of bodybuilders and I enjoy the meatier variety of stocky men, this particular meaty, muscular combination is my nirvana. I've been known to follow them down the street for a few blocks, just to take one in. It's a reflection of my own personal religion in praise of the big, black ass.

At the bar that night, I chatted and flirted with my new friend, dying to get a look at his butt. Not wanting to be too forward, I bided my time with the rest of his enjoyable presence, which included a nice personality. Finally he said he had to take a piss and I was giddy at that thought of being able to watch him walk away. As he turned toward the can, the sight was the unimaginable answer to all of my ass prayers. Even beneath fairly loose jeans, he had one of the most spectacular butts I'd ever seen. It was high, wide and round, almost absurdly protruding from his back and legs—both of which looked nice, too. It had that gravity-defying quality characteristic of a truly great ass. I must have gone into a trance because the next thing I knew, he was walking back toward me with a puzzled look in his eyes.

"Everything okay?"

"Um, yeah, sure, why?" I tried to act cool.

"You had this weird look on your face."

I decided to come clean. "Well, to be honest, I was admiring your ass on the way to the bathroom and, well, um, it just kinda took my breath away."

He smiled, a full acknowledgement of what he had and the power that came with it.

"I'm a big ass fan," I said, beaming at him.

"I've got a big ass that loves its fans."

I laughed. "So I suppose that if one were to hook up with you, a lot of attention would need to be paid to the extraordinary ass."

"You got that right."

"Well, I'd like to officially put in my application as service attendant."

"Cool," he said, "your application is accepted."

We made our way out of the bar and I tried to stay a half step behind him. He stopped under a street light, which gave me my best view yet, and turned around.

"Stop straggling," he said. "You'll get plenty of chances to look at my ass."

I grabbed the first cab I saw. Neither of us said a word on the way back to my place. I could taste the excitement that only comes from the thrill of uncharted territory ... the moment before fantasy becomes reality.

We arrived at my apartment and he went into the bathroom to take a leak, pulling down his pants just enough to reveal the top of a jockstrap. There are few ways to better showcase a bubble butt than with a jock. It frames the cheeks lovingly, presenting them as an altar upon which acts of reverence will be performed.

After he finished, he turned his head and said, "Like what you see?" This guy was clearly attuned to the effect of his ass—a maestro with a Stradivarius.

"Hell yes!" I replied.

He pulled up his pants but left them unbuttoned. He came to me and grabbed me and gave me a deep kiss. My hands cupped his ass as if I would otherwise drown. Still kissing, I pulled him into the bedroom, his hands all over my body, my hands firmly grasping that ass. Even through his jeans, that ass felt amazing. I never wanted to let go.

When we bumped into my bed, he pulled away and told me to sit down. I did so, anxiously awaiting his next move. There are some men with great asses who either aren't aware of their effect or are too insecure to revel in it. This man was neither. As if on cue, he turned around and pushed out his ass, the top of the jockstrap reappearing. He shook his ass and wiggled it around. I was like a straight guy at a tatty bar, mouth agape, anticipating. The mysteries of that butt were about to be revealed.

Slowly he drew down his pants, each inch revealing more and more of that extraordinary ass. The side straps of the jock came into view, pushing his ass toward the center, as if there was so much ass, it couldn't be contained. He had full round curves that truly put the bubble in bubble butt. The complexion of his ass, like the rest of him, was creamy milk chocolate and completely smooth, providing no distractions from its exquisiteness.

He continued to gyrate his ass as he lowered his pants. It

had a hypnotic effect; my head tracked the circular motion. He reached the bottom of his bottom, offering up the full bounty on display, and I suddenly snapped back, startled by the view. With his pants just below his jock-strapped globes, he turned around and smiled, acknowledging my worshipful gaze. He shuffled his feet back toward me until that butt was inches from my face. I gasped and whispered, "Oh, my God!"

The proximity had my mind spinning, unable to comprehend the glory of what was before me. I took in every inch from this closer vantage point, now able to get a whiff of his personal musk. It was every bit as intoxicating as himself and his ass.

"Go ahead," he whispered, "feel it."

I was so drunk with its effects that feeling it hadn't even occurred to me. That's how magnificent his ass was. I continued to stare for a moment, then lifted my hands and gently placed them on his cheeks. Electrifying. As if I had discovered the secret of life. His cheeks were so warm and full, my hands were unable to wrap completely around them. I marveled at their strength and then squeezed them—like Mr. Whipple with the forbidden Charmin—finding they possessed just enough give to make my knees go weak. Thankfully, I was still seated. I continued to feel them as if I were checking out melons at the store, carefully appraising each one for its ripeness. In the fog of my reverie, I heard slight moans. I thought: if just feeling them was eliciting this kind of reaction from him, we're really in for a good time.

"You like that?" I asked. "You like it when someone feels up that butt?"

"Oh, yeah, man," he groaned back. "You know I love that, especially from a real ass lover."

"You've got the right man for the job, baby, 'cause that ass deserves to be loved."

"Then love it, motherfucker. That ass needs some love."

As if ordered from the Temple Mount, I snapped into action. I grabbed that ass more firmly, feeling it, slapping it. I took control of his butt. He moaned even louder. I pushed him forward to display that ass even better. It spread out farther. Through the depth of his cheeks, I could see his hole peeking through. I rubbed my face over every inch of his cheeks, kissing and offering the occasional slap. His moaning only encouraged me.

"C'mon, baby, show me you love that ass. Take care of that big, chocolate butt."

I pulled down his jockstrap and told him to step out of his pants. He turned and I was presented with another delightful surprise—his long, thick, big-headed dick with its inviting, pro-nounced upward curve. It was hard and dripping, demanding attention. I couldn't let this surprise go to waste. I locked my lips on the head and grabbed his cheeks, holding on for dear life. As he held my head, I dipped my fingers into the deep crevice between his cheeks. It was warm with just a flutter of hair.

I pulled his dick out of my mouth to take a breath and I looked up at my man, who was clearly as heated as I was. I sat back and took in the beauty of his entire body in profile: the big strong arms, the meaty pecs, the torso that tapered downward to his ass, the sturdy, muscular thighs that led up to his ass. And, of course, that big, hard, dripping dick that completed the package. From head to toe, he was the perfect man.

Our eyes locked. I grabbed his thighs and slowly started the climb north. Though I was tempted to go back down on his dick, I turned him around and urged him toward the bed. He knew exactly what to do. He assumed one of the all-time great ass positions—down on all fours, face in the bed. Again, I had to take it in for a moment, to study it, knowing it would soon be an indelible image in mind. He reached back and pulled apart his cheeks, eliciting yet another in a continuing series of gasps from my lips.

But those lips had even better things to do.

I pushed his hands away, grabbed his cheeks and dove in face first. At last, those hot globes were wrapped around my face and my nose was buried in his pucker. I took a nice long whiff, inhaling his sweet nectar. It felt like an extraordinary act, being buried in his ass, those big cheeks enveloping my face as I pushed them inward, creating nothing for me to feel and breathe in but his ass. As the initial rush wore off, I pulled back and looked at his hole. It, too, was perfect. A pronounced ring with a puckered rosebud—just right.

I wrapped my mouth around the hole and sucked it in, still fondling his cheeks, never wanting to let go. I made out with that hole like an ex-con seeing his first woman in ten years. I licked around the edge, tasted the insides, then slobbered up and down the crack. I rubbed that hole all over my face, feeling him shudder when my goatee massaged it. His response was almost as good as his ass.

"Yes, baby, eat that damn hole! Lemma feel that tongue deep inside me! Suck the motherfuckin' life outta that hole!"

I plunged my tongue deeper and deeper, trying to pull those big cheeks back as far as I could. I needed a different position, though, to get maximum penetration. To his great displeasure, I slipped my tongue out of his hole and told him to stand up. His displeasure was short-lived, though, when I lay down on the bed, with my head toward the edge and uttered the asslover's rally cry:

"Sit on my face!"

Slowly he lowered the mother lode. The view was exquisite. His thighs disappeared; his cheeks pulled apart to reveal that beautiful hole, still wet from my tonguing. Light turned to dark. I instinctively stuck out my tongue, feeling for his hole. The sensation was like no other and I gladly would've stayed there for the rest of my life.

I found his hole with my tongue and plunged in, feeling him control the movement as he shifted and lowered his ass. As any committed ass-eater knows, this allows your tongue to work more efficiently, sharing the work load. I was able to both suck his hole rabidly and plunge my tongue deeper. The thickness of my tongue reached its limit as he began to ride my face. My hands alternated from his thighs to his dick to, naturally, his ass. He rode my face in a steady rhythm, allowing my tongue to move around and find his hot spots—those lovely places that elicit the deepest gasps and moans. As I learned of them, I was able to work them and him into a frenzy.

I couldn't get enough of his ass riding my face, those big, strong thighs straddling my head, those beautiful brown cheeks wrapping around my face and that delicious hole opening more and more as my tongue dug deeper and deeper. I loved the pliable but strong ring of his pucker as it loosened to allow my penetration.

Suddenly, I felt the need to play with that hole more directly. I lifted him up from my face, to which he responded with a
mournful grunt. I pushed him back onto the bed and folded him
in half, exposing that glistening hole in the middle of his wide-
spread cheeks. He was smiling again, knowing he would soon be
back in ecstasy.

I took a few good licks before I began to run my finger
around the pucker, gently teasing him with it. His big dick was
rock hard, which added to the visual pleasure. He looked at me
with pleading eyes, emitting a barely-heard whimper. Occasionally I'd lean down and suck on his hole while pushing my finger
into it. His whimpers became moans when I pushed farther into
his warm supple asshole. It felt like heaven. I worked my finger
around, discovering more hot spots along the way, until I hit the
Big Kahuna. As my finger traced against his prostate, he moaned
loudly and his dripping dick jumped.

I pushed my finger in farther into his hole and slapped his
ass cheeks. I loved watching his face react and hearing his con-
stant stream of encouragement to dig deeper. I plunged my finger fully in and took his dripping dick in my mouth and fixed my
eyes on him. He looked like a man possessed, pleading with me
not to stop. I moved my finger in and out, then added a second
digit, getting a similarly enthusiastic response. His pre-cum
oozed into my mouth. In and out my fingers went, caressing his
warmth, feeling his essence. It was like a holy ritual, creating
comfort and joy, reassuring me that this was where I was meant
to be, that he and his ass were worthy of my worship.

His hole was opening up beautifully, so I added a third finger. He responded by pushing his ass back to my hand frantical-

ly, as if he couldn't get enough. He pushed himself up, keeping my fingers inside him, and squatted down, applying greater pressure into his hole. As he rode up and down, I sucked his dick.

His ass practically assaulted my three fingers. This hole was hungry, so I tried to put a fourth up there. But it wasn't to be—three was his limit. Nonetheless, I remained committed to the digits already being fucked mercilessly by his warm, wet hole. Watching this man ride my hand was a sight to behold. I felt as if I controlled the center of his universe.

I continued to suck his cock, concentrating on his big, thick head. His movement became more frenetic.

"Fuck that hole, baby. Oh, my fuckin' God!"

I pumped away, reveling in the extraordinary feeling of having this man ride my hand with such enormous ferocity. Suddenly, he went quiet. I felt his ass open to its greatest capacity yet. He then pulled his dick out of my mouth, screamed like a banshee and came all over my face. He collapsed onto my hand, but I didn't want to let go. He lay back as I slowly moved my fingers around inside him. "Just keep 'em in there for a little bit, 'kay?"

No problem there. I looked at him, bathed in afterglow, his dick less hard but still swollen. His eyes were closed, but he was smiling slyly.

"Damn, that was good," he uttered."

Who's he tellin'? I thought to myself.

He and his butt were the manifestation of all of that's good and pure and true in this world. A man and his butt. Or more specifically, a man, his butt and me. But this man and this butt were worthy of praise in the truest sense. He was the new messiah of my religion, in service and praise of the big, black ass.

Bluejay

ROBINMAN

Bluejay leapt from the ledge and flew in the air for four heart-beats before landing on the ledge on the other side of the alley. His powerful legs took up the impact, allowing him to spring ahead like a racehorse. The caped boy had been running across the Centropolis skyline for 20 minutes straight and was barely breathing hard. Such athletic exertion was literally child's play to him. The men he pursued were not so trained or dedicated, but they had a long head start.

He spotted two of the four men, running and stumbling across the rooftops, fleeing in blind panic. To his left, the masked teen caught a glimpse of the other two, one of which was already pitching forward in exhaustion while the second seemed to glide along. This man was the leader and Bluejay marked him as someone to watch. These two first, the boy thought. He veered to the right, did a handstand off an air conditioning unit and dropped in front of the two thieves. His blue-gloved fist flashed out and crushed the first man's nose. The thief was knocked off his feet by the powerful blow, and fell to the rooftop, screaming and clutching his nose in pain. The second man dodged to one side, causing the boy's kick to miss him, then swung at Bluejay's head with the heavy bag of money. Bluejay blocked the bag with one hand, then lashed out with a right cross to the thief's jaw—once, then twice. The man crumbled to the ground, unconscious while Bluejay shot off after the second pair.

One thief was laid up behind a stairwell entrance, panting and clutching his leather valise. The boy clad in blue leapt up, swung on a projecting bar and dropped down in front of the man as the thief gave a panting whine.

Bluejay was a sleek and lean 18 year-old boy, dressed in a costume that looked as if it had been spray-painted onto his whipcord-muscled, well-defined physique: a medium blue bodysuit with dark blue trunks and indigo leather gloves and boots. A short, hip-length indigo cape fell off his broad shoulders, the trailing edge cut so that it looked like the wings of a giant bird. The boy was handsome to the point of beauty, only the strong line of his jaw saving his face from a pretty, androgynous look. His eyes—behind the dark blue mask—were bright cornflower blue and his short hair was the color of summer sunshine.

The thief cringed, anticipating a beating. But the youth flashed a bright smile instead. Two capsules tumbled from his gloved hand and fell onto the rooftop. Billowing gas erupted and sent the thief into dreamland. Bluejay waited for the cloud to dissipate, then opened the leather valise. Green and silver circuit boards glittered in the reflected light and Bluejay frowned. These were not your ordinary thieves. High tech equipment like this was useless unless you knew where to fence it, and from the looks of them, these men wouldn't know how to fence a stolen lollipop, much less top-of-the-line microcircuits.

Redhawk—his mentor, partner and older half of their crime-fighting duo—would want to know about this. The 18 year-old boy took off like a shot once more, eager to get the last man and find out what was going on here. Tomorrow morning, he'd be back at Centropolis University as Ricky Dane, typical college freshman. Tonight, though, he could blow off steam and bust some criminal heads. He sprinted across the darkened rooftops of the city's Black Harbor district. The last thief was probably heading for some kind of rendezvous or hideout, so Bluejay would follow at a distance, let the creep think he was home free.

Eventually, the man disappeared down an open skylight. Seconds later, Bluejay somersaulted onto a crate next to it, then jumped through the skylight and landed on the cold floor of the darkened warehouse. He narrowed his eyes, waiting for a shot or a blow. Nothing. The youth turned. The last thief was standing directly behind him. He was wearing a black eye mask, but Ricky could tell the man was handsome with smooth delicate features and beautiful green eyes. Eyes you could fall into. His black hair had blue highlights and fell across his forehead. He was dressed in midnight blue from head to toe, revealing a lean, breathtakingly symmetrical body with perfectly defined muscles. His gloved hands had long, delicate fingers that ended in short, sharp claws. His boots were similarly clawed.

No wonder he could climb like that.

Bluejay swallowed and stepped back as the man approached. The man was barely older than himself, maybe in his early 20s. He stepped back again, staring into the thief's green eyes, until he hit something. A thick metal support beam. He turned back to face the man, whose face was now an inch from his own—those wonderful eyes so wide and compelling. Bluejay let out an unsteady breath. He should be fighting this guy, retrieving the stolen boards. His hands clenched into fists, then slowly uncurled. He could smell the man's sweet breath, he was so close.

"We do not have to fight," the young man said in a soft French accent. His claw-like gloved hand pushed a soft crescent of hair out of Bluejay's eyes. Bluejay was frozen. The masked thief reached behind Bluejay's neck and gently scratched the skin there, a sharp stinging pain that disappeared almost as soon as it started. Bluejay felt a wave of dizziness rush through him. He swayed on his feet, confused and hesitant.

The young man smiled and kissed the boy hero softly on the lips. Once, twice, the thief tasted him, then the man's tongue slipped past Ricky's lips and the kiss became an exploration. Bluejay closed his eyes, relaxing against the pillar, letting the man kiss him. The thief's touch was gentle, sliding over Bluejay's deep chest and sculpted arms, up to his long neck and soft cheeks. The thief undid Bluejay's short cape and let it fall to the ground, then he slid off the boy's tunic, revealing his powerful golden-muscled torso.

They kissed for several minutes, the young man's tongue sliding into Bluejay's passive mouth over and over again until finally they parted. Bluejay licked his lips and moaned. He was panting and his young cock was a rigid piece of iron in his silky trunks. The thief nibbled at his ear. "I am Le Panthère," he said, almost whispering. "You see, pretty Bluejay, we do not have to fight." He pulled back to look at the boy's angelic face. "You are the most beautiful boy in the world," the thief said, then kissed the end of Bluejay's nose. His hands slid over Bluejay's chest and arms. "The poison on my gloves will ... confuse you. It makes people pliant, very susceptible to my suggestions and my desires." Le Panthère kissed the handsome teen again, and laughed. "You will do anything for me."

Bluejay found himself nodding, his bright blue eyes blinking in confusion behind his mask. Le Panthère drew his clawed fingers down Bluejay's chest, leaving soft white lines that faded. Bluejay's head fell back as the man teased his nipples—turning them into to stiff nubs—then traced the well-defined muscles of his abdomen. The two masked youths embraced, kissing passionately. Bluejay shivered, feeling the thief's lean hard body against his stronger frame, and moved his hips, pressing his rigid enclosed cock against the warmth he could feel in the other man's costume. Le Panthère bit Bluejay gently on the ear, shivering himself in desire and delight. "You are wonderful," the thief moaned.

Le Panthère knelt, taking Bluejay with him, and pinned the bare-chested boy on the ground. He laughed and the young hero beneath him smiled. Le Panthère straddled the blue-masked boy and scooted back so he could slowly remove Bluejay's trunks and undo his tights. Bluejay's cock sprang out into the open air. The thief grabbed it, wrapped his hand around the shaft and took the red cockhead between his soft wet lips.

"Dude!" Bluejay gasped. "Dude!"

Le Panthère laughed and stood up, pulling Bluejay with him. Bluejay grabbed an iron bar to steady himself. Le Panthère laughed softly to himself, then pulled a chain from a shelf. Gently he bound Bluejay to the iron bar above him, pulling the youth's muscled arms up and to the sides. Bluejay swayed in his makeshift pillory, unsure why he was letting himself be bound this way. Le Panthère pulled off Bluejay's weapons belt, his boots and at last, his tights. Then the handsome thief moved behind the captive and kissed the back of the boy's neck. "Now, my pretty bird-boy, I have you."

Le Panthère knelt and slid his gloved hands up Bluejay's powerful legs, finally coming to that object of his ultimate desire, the boy hero's beautiful ass. It was trim, two pert firm mounds of muscle that curved into his legs and melted up into his back. Two dimples showed, the result of years of working out and hard, punishing exercise. Le Panthère traced the dimples and the boy's ass twitched in response. It twitched again when the handsome thief planted a gentle kiss on the soft pale skin.

"Ooh," came from Bluejay. He struggled against the chains and bit his lip. Le Panthère kissed the boy's ass again and again, then licked the milk-pale, baby-soft skin.

"So wonderful." The thief parted Bluejay's ass and Bluejay sighed as he felt the man's hot breath on his twitching little pucker. Then the masked boy closed his eyes and bit his lip again as he felt Le Panthère's soft lips kiss his most private place. Le Panthère kissed the tender pink flesh over and over, gentle wet kisses that drove Bluejay wild. A pearly drop of precum oozed out of the boy's plum-red cockhead and slid down the veined shaft until it disappeared into the sun-golden fur of his groin.

Another followed it, then another, until Bluejay felt a regular stream of his dick-honey wet his groin, then trickle down his muscled legs.

The thief coated the tips of two fingers with the precum and pressed them to Bluejay's opening, teasing his index finger past the firm muscle. The finger sank deep into the heat of Bluejay's body and the bound teen tensed, muscles bulging erotically as the chains were tested once more.

"Stop it, please," the masked hero groaned. "Don't … ooohhh!"

The chains chimed as the boy writhed in his makeshift prison. The thief penetrated with the second finger, pushing deep into his little boy pussy. Bluejay cried out as a third finger joined the pair, stretching his tight hole until a light sheen of sweat covered the boy's back. Le Panthère glided his other hand over the youth's marble-hard thighs and legs, tanned to a soft gold color save for the pale white lines that showed off the hero's ass. The thief combed through the boy's golden cock bush, then toyed with his low-hanging balls. He touched, caressed and gently squeezed the smooth ball sac, tightening his grip until Bluejay twisted in discomfort. Then it was on to the rock-hard boycock jutting out from Bluejay's groin. It was smooth and cut, the shaft nicely veined while the plum-red helmet was swollen and smooth as silk. Le Panthère caressed the cockhead and Bluejay trembled in his chains.

"God, please, let me cum," the masked boy moaned.

"Not yet, *mon bel amoureux.*" The thief continued to play with the boy's ass before finally removing his fingers and letting the youth relax for a moment. "So wonderful," Le Panthère sighed as he kissed Bluejay's quivering hole. The boy's gates opened and the thief's tongue penetrated Bluejay with a warm gentle pressure that caused the boy's head to snap back. A moan escaped Bluejay's lips, then a soft cry as his cock squirted a little more lube into the cold air.

"Holy shit," the masked hero moaned, shaking his head from side to side, sweat flying from his hair in a glistening halo. The thief plunged into Bluejay's tight little hole with his tongue, then pulled back. Bluejay relaxed then stiffened again as the wet fluid tongue was replaced by a long rigid finger. The boy yipped and pulled at his restraints. The digit gently but insistently penetrated him, up and up until it brushed his prostate. Bluejay moaned softly and the thief suddenly laughed.

"You are no stranger to this, no?" The man stood up, undid a flap in his one-piece costume and let his long dark cock plop against Bluejay's back.

"God, you're long," said the masked teen. "You'll kill me if you put that in me."

Le Panthère embraced the chained boy from behind, sliding his long thick member against the pink fold of the teen's ass. He nibbled on Bluejay's ear and neck. "What, you do not want me to claim your pretty pussy, little bird? I bet that you are very used to this. You are no struggling virgin. You respond too well for you to be so fresh."

"Take me," said Bluejay. The boy closed his eyes and cried out as the thief's mancock invaded him.

"Take that up your little boy pussy," the thief grunted. He began to piston his cock into the helpless hero, grinning as Bluejay's high-pitched cries echoed from the bare walls. Sweat trickled down the thief's face until finally he grunted and began to pump the boy full of cum.

"Aaahh!" cried Bluejay, arching his back as he felt the hot gush in his ass, then his own rigid boycock unloading. Long ropes of cum squirted from his dick, landing on the warehouse floor.

When both were done, Le Panthère slowly pulled his cock from the tired boy's ass. Then the masked boy felt the man's fingers at his rosebud once more, pulling him open again. Then there was that marvelous tongue. The man cleaned him thoroughly, until his twitching pussy was fresh once more.

Next the man stood up in front of him, cupped Bluejay's angelic face in his hands and kissed the boy again, a deep passionate kiss that let the teen taste the salt of the thief's cum and the subtle tang of his own tight ass. Bluejay tried to keep kissing, but the man pulled away.

"No, no, sweet one," he purred, straightening the captive boy's hair. "We will meet again, Bluejay, I am sure of that. You will remember this night, no?" He brushed his lips across Bluejay's soft cheek. "You will free yourself soon, mon ami,"

Le Panthère faded into the darkness of the warehouse. Bluejay hung by the chains until he was sure the man was gone, then, with a quick snap and twist, he was free. Redhawk, his mentor and partner in crime fighting, had shown him how to get out of such simple bonds when he was still a kid in short pants.

Bluejay winced as he felt his violated ass. He closed his eyes and probed it, sliding a finger in, then back out.

Yeah, the boy thought, we'll meet again.

He smiled, gathered his costume and started to dress.

And next time, I will be on top.

No Hole Like the Present

WES BERLIN

He pushed the lips out. They flayed open like an unfurling red rose. I playfully jabbed the tips of my fingers into the pouting flesh. The lips grabbed hold of them and slowly drew them in. I'd been fisting him for nearly two hours and he still had magnificent control.

"It drives me crazy when you tease my hole that way," he whispered, peering up from the improvised playpen on his living room floor.

It drives me crazy knowing how good it makes him feel.

I pushed my hand deeper. His jaw dropped and his eyes rolled back inside his head. He was in sexual nirvana. I found myself admiring his glistening torso, dark swollen nipples and impressive slab of cut meat which he was vigorously pulling. His body was long, lean and naturally smooth, his toned chest and taut biceps the results of near-religious devotion to daily workouts.

But best of all, at that moment, he was all mine.

He had enormous capacity. I'd been two-handing his hole for what seemed like hours, pushing in deeper, first with one fist, then the other, pounding and pumping. He was taking it all and begging for more. I was in nearly up to the elbow. He said if we played long enough, I could go in farther. I varied tempos. He liked it rough and he liked it gentle. When I quick-punched in and out, he whimpered with pleasure. To run into him in an everyday setting, you'd never guess in a million years that this clean-cut preppy boy had a butt hole that could practically suck up a hockey stick. Why had it taken so long for us to get back together? We were obviously very compatible.

It'd been nearly three years since we first met on one of the hardcore phone lines. I'd put on my usual message—looking for some sweet hungry hole to lick and stretch—and he had replied. I liked his description: late twenties, in-shape and a willing bottom. When I opened the door, I was not disappointed and hoped he wasn't either. It was a Friday evening, early fall; he wore a light windbreaker and carried a backpack. He came into the apartment and I ushered him into the bedroom. I'd created a makeshift play area on my bed with a green army surplus blanket and old bath towels.

"Is that your party blanket?" he asked, sounding cocky. He knew he was pretty hot and could say what he wanted. I decided to let it go.

There was very little foreplay. He was all business—as so

many bottoms can be. He was there to be opened and stretched
and that was the focus. He had play rules, he announced. No
touching his cock with the same hand I'd been fisting him with
and no touching my cock and using that hand to go up his ass.
He wanted me to use Crisco going into his hole but preferred I
use Lube or KY to manipulate myself. He'd brought rubber
gloves in case I didn't have any. In these times of fatal infections,
you respect a man's wishes.

We played for a couple of hours. He really liked it rough
and the harder I punched his hole, the more it turned him on.
We both shot big loads. It was barely eleven o'clock. He said he
was going to hit a couple of the leather bars and see if he could
find some more action. I was just as glad to call it a night.

After that, we tried to get together on several occasions but
kept missing each other. I was traveling, he was working over-
time, he had visitors, I wasn't in the mood. Weeks stretched into
months and we gradually stopped phoning. I chalked it up to
what might have been.

Then, a few days ago, I was on the raunch line and heard his
voice again.

"By the way," he said eventually, "we already know each
other. We played once before. You knew me as Don."

At that point, I didn't give a damn what his name was if he
was as hot as his stats and/or the guy I remembered. I was ready
to cut to the chase.

"So what're you up to today, Don?"

"Not much."

"Let's play!"

I looked forward to dipping into that hole that was quite

gifted. The prospect of penetrating an anal cavity in a myriad of ways, as well as the actual act itself, sets my horny-mones in motion. I've always been drawn to the shape of a man's buttocks and am notorious for turning to look back at a guy's behind after passing him on the street. A lot of straight guys don't know what's going on and instinctively check to see if they still have their wallets.

I prefer naturally smooth or shaved holes, but I've experienced the joys of hairy ones as well, especially when the pubes are soft and downy. And I've done lots of guys who have superb control, who are able to push out their lips at will or skillfully suck in a throbbing penis, fist, forearm or gigantic dildo with equal élan. I've seen holes that could take two man-sized cocks at once, or gobble a string of rubber or metal balls. The more practiced the hole, the more it turns me on. (I often wonder what's going through the head of a fisting bottom. He is no doubt in charge even if he lets you take control. He calls the shots but also gets maximum pleasure. A willing receptacle who is taking the larger risk, being at one's most vulnerable and strongest at the same time.)

Now, in the midst of our long-awaited rematch, the versatility and impressive capacity of Don's full-service butt hole contributed greatly to my desire to satisfy him. He was a beautiful man with a beautiful hole that he wanted used to the best of one's creative limits and I did my best to oblige. He seemed happy enough, but in a moment of self-doubt, I asked if he wanted to bring out some of his toys. He demurred.

It was time to give myself some relief. I announced I was taking off one of the gloves to play with myself. He was about to remind me of his rule but stopped himself when I dutifully reached for the Lube dispenser and squirted a gob in my hand. Now I had one hand tanking his greedy hole and the other beating my rock hard meat.

"I want to fuck you!" I handed him a condom to open. He did so and rolled it down my hard slick prick. I pulled my other hand out of his ass and raised his legs onto my shoulders. I mounted him in one smooth plunge. He was warm and slippery. Amazingly, he still had enough elasticity to grab my cock, which to be quite honest, is no baseball bat. I rode in and out of his well-greased pit. His solid thighs pressed against my chest with every thrust. We were face-to-face—mouths nearly touching, smelling each other's breath—but never once kissed. Before I could stop myself, I began shooting and shouted, "I'm cumming" in case he wanted to join me. He increased the hand action on his own cock and spurts of milky jizz ripped out, some hitting my stomach. We collapsed into each other's arms in a moment of sublime orgasmic exhaustion.

I pulled out slowly, discarded the condom and stretched my stiffened joints. I washed up and dressed and started making dinner plans in my head. He slipped into some jeans and an unbuttoned shirt and began picking up the play area. Neither of us wanted to linger.

"Great hole," I said as he opened the door.

"Come back," he said.

"Will do," I said, but had the feeling it was going to be a while before we played again.

But then, I could be wrong.

Bottom Floor

JONATHAN ASCHE

He got on at the eighth floor. I was the only other person on the elevator. He smiled and nodded as he stepped inside. I mechanically copied his greeting, hypnotized by his glistening green eyes, his full lips, his strong jaw. As my gaze drifted downward, I saw that the body was worthy of the face: broad shoulders and full pecs strained the fabric of his pale blue Oxford shirt; his tailored gray pants hung neatly from his narrow waist, the generous pleats unable to hide the swinging of his cock.

Then he turned around to face the buttons beside the door, pressing the one for the first floor. I wondered if he heard my sudden intake of breath or sensed my staring as my eyes went to his ass. I licked my lips as I admired that high, round butt that stretched the seat of his pants tight, making his conservative corporate uniform sexy. So sexy, that in the time it took for us to ride from the eighth to the seventh floor I'd sprung a massive hard-on.

The elevator stopped on the sixth floor. A crowd of people flooded in, forcing the Guy With the Perfect Ass to move backward. As the crowd packed and redistributed itself, he took another step, moving even closer to me. One more step and he was against me, his shoulder blades pressing into my chest, his plush, bubble butt resting against my boner. Simultaneously, I experienced a flush of embarrassment and an even greater surge of excitement. Naturally, I expected this contact with the nameless object of my lust to be brief. He would jump forward, startled, mumble an "excuse me" and we'd both pretend my raging hard-on never happened.

Instead, he stayed where he was. While all the other passengers faced the front of the elevator, eyes focused on the digital read-out of the floors as we descended, the hunky young executive leaned back a little more, suffocating my throbbing rod with the weight of his perfectly-shaped ass. I inhaled sharply, getting a whiff of his clean hair and woodsy cologne. Neither of us spoke. We'd established a more thrilling line of communication.

As we passed the fifth floor, he began to squeeze that God-given butt against me. No, make that *grind* against me. He acted nonchalant about it, staring straight ahead with the other junior executives and secretaries, while rotating his hips in a slow, deliberate fashion, massaging my cock with his ass. It was all I could do not to reach around that narrow waist of his and start pulling at his zipper.

By the time we got to the second floor, my cock was aching and my shorts were soaked with pre-cum. This guy would not stop grinding his ass against me. I heard two women giggle nervously. Had they noticed us? I was too turned on to give a shit.

When the elevator stopped at the first floor, the doors opened and the crowd pushed its way into the lobby. I saw one woman looking back at me, covering her mouth as she giggled. I looked away, back at this hot stranger who'd been pressing his ass against me for the entire ride. He stepped forward. Was this where we parted company? Not if I could help it. I opened my mouth to speak, to say—what?—but a croak rumbled in my throat. The Guy With the Perfect Ass looked back at me, saw the lust in my eyes and the tent pitched in my gray pants and flashed his equally perfect teeth. He walked up to the panel of buttons, pressed B for basement and the doors closed. When the doors opened again, he stepped out and I followed.

We went down the yellow-gray corridor into a no-man's land of supply closets and mail rooms. He tried a door marked "storage," discovered it was unlocked and we stepped into the cramped little room stacked floor-to-ceiling with boxes of files.

The door was barely shut behind us before he was loosening his belt and unzipping his fly. He was about to yank his pants down, show me his stiff prick, but I stopped him. "Turn around," I said, my voice low and raspy. He did as I said, then pulled his pants down. My cock pulsed as he exposed his full, creamy white globes separated by deep crack. He leaned forward, putting his hands against the wall and pushing his ass out toward me. My heart hammered in my chest. I sank to my knees. My trembling hands caressed the smooth, fleshy hills of his ass, eventually pulling his butt cheeks apart to get a view of his dark valley. The crack of his ass had a light dusting of fur, with a ring of coarser, darker hairs surrounding his little rosebud. His ass-ring peeked out from its fuzzy border, its tan lips puckered in anticipation.

I leaned forward, sinking my face into the crevice of his butt, the cheeks of his butt rubbing against the cheeks of my face. My nose was filled with his scent: clean, yet still tinged with that sharp, manly musk that no soap can obliterate entirely. My tongue blindly sought out his tender hole, gently touching the tiny folds of skin around his sphincter. He moaned as I lapped at his asshole, teasing the sensitive orifice with my warm, wet tongue. Abruptly, I pulled my face away. Hooking my thumbs in the crack of his ass, I pulled his ass-lips apart. The stranger gasped. I studied the dime-sized opening, looking at the rose-hued flesh at the inner walls of his butthole that faded into a black abyss. I toyed with the rim of his open hole, circling it with the tip of my index finger, whispering a breathy "oh, yeah" so he knew that I was pleased with what I saw.

I rammed my tongue up his ass.

He moaned loudly. My tongue dove deep, wiggling about in his velvety hole. If people were in the hall outside, they could've heard us, but his moaning and groaning excited me more, urged me to plunge my tongue deeper into his ass. "Oh, yeah, eat it," the Stranger With the Perfect Ass panted. "Eat my ass!" He rotated his hips, grinding his ass against my face like he was grinding it against my crotch in the elevator—only this time more intense. He was bucking and gyrating, reaching one hand back to grab a fistful of my hair, pulling my face forward, urging my tongue even deeper into his ass. I clamped my hands on his thighs, pulling his butt against my face like I was trying to stuff my entire head through his asshole.

I pulled my face away just long enough to stick my index

finger in my mouth, coating it with spit. I slid it into the stranger's hole. His sphincter clamped down on it, holding it there, relaxing slightly when I begin to slowly rotate my finger inside him. I returned my fingers to my mouth, adding the middle finger this time. I pushed the two spit-lubed fingers to the mystery man's asshole, stretching it a little wider, eliciting a tiny whimper from him. When his ass got used to the second digit, I added a third. He sucked in his breath, hissing between clenched teeth as I slid three fingers into his moist insides, the dime-sized hole now a silver dollar. I could tell I was testing his endurance, but he didn't tell me to stop.

With my other hand I fumbled with my belt and zipper, struggling to free my aching cock. This was long overdue. My drawers were soaked with pre-cum and my prick was almost purple, it was so desperate for release. It vibrated when I touched it, squeezing out a drop of crystalline dew.

"I want to fuck you so bad," I growled, gripping the base of my cock with one hand, toying with his ass with the other.

There was a complication, though: Neither of us had a rubber. No problem. Pulling my fingers out of his ass, I got to my feet and pushed my pants and underwear down my thighs until they fell down to my ankles. I spit into my palm and lubed up my dick, although it hardly seemed necessary with all the pre-come coating it. I used another gob of spit to lubricate his ass, just for good measure. Then I pushed my cock against this stranger's butt, letting my boner sink into the warm channel of his ass-cheeks.

I began rubbing my cock up and down, the soft skin of his butt-cheeks caressing it. I pressed against him, hard, pushing my throbbing cock against this sexy stranger's asshole but not pene-trating it. I really wanted to shove my dick into his hole, but this felt pretty good. Damn good. He liked it, too. The Guy With the Perfect Ass started grinding against me. His ass bobbed against my cock, countering my own thrusts. I leaned over his back and whis-pered into his ear, my voice a lusty rumble, telling him how hot his ass was, how good it felt against my cock. The stranger just pant-ed and moaned in response. When I reached around his waist and grabbed his thick, hard dick, his moans got even louder.

The sensation of my cock sliding in his butt crack became too much to bear. I was dizzy with pleasure. Each time I thrust my prick upward, each time the hunky stranger pushed his ass back against my cock, I'd feel my ball-sac get a bit tighter as my nuts got ready to fire their heavy load. Suddenly, a white-hot tin-gle rippled across every nerve ending in my body. "I'm … gonna … shoot!" I groaned between choked breaths, releasing my load. Thick, white ribbons of my jizz splattered onto his ass and the tail of his shirt.

I practically melted against the guy, whoever he was. It was one of the most powerful orgasms I'd had in recent memory, taking all my strength with it. Yet even though I wanted to col-lapse onto the floor, I knew my mystery man still needed to get off—and I knew just where I wanted to be when that happened.

I got back on my knees, eye-level with those succulent globes of flesh, now frosted with my own creamy load. I had made quite an impressive mess, and I intended to clean it up. Bringing my face to the man's full butt, I lapped up my own splooge until not a drop was left—save that on his shirt tail; let his dry cleaner take care of that. When his cheeks were clean, I

moved into the crack of his ass to tongue his hole. As my tongue
slithered inside him, my hand reached between his legs to grab
my fuck buddy's boner. I swear I could feel it swell to my touch.
I pushed my tongue into his moist hole, wiggling it around
inside while I pulled on his dick. He writhed, his body twisting
and shimmying as I tongue-fucked him. In seconds he shot his
wad, his sticky come hitting the moss-green wall.

When I got to my feet, I spun this anonymous hunk around
and kissed him. As our tongues twisted together, I reached down
to squeeze his ass one more time.

"By the way," I said, "my name's Jay."

"I'm Tom," he replied, hiking his pants up over his hips.

We left the storage room, a bit disheveled but quite satisfied. As we got onto the elevator, I asked if I could call him some-
time. Tom didn't say anything, just pulled a card out of his wallet and a pen from his pocket. As the elevator traveled upward I
saw him write something on the card. When he was done, the
Guy With the Perfect Ass whose name was Tom turned to me
and I reached out to take the card. But he moved past my hand,
pushing himself against me and sliding his hand down the front
of my pants, leaving his card in the waistband of my shorts. The
elevator stopped and Tom jumped back. Three women got on
the elevator, abruptly ending our contact. He got off at the
eighth floor, looking back at me and nodding before he stepped
off the elevator.

When I got to my floor I immediately went to the men's
room. Sequestered in a stall, I unzipped my pants and reached
inside my briefs to retrieve Tom's card. I smiled as I read it.

"Next time," he'd written, "bring condoms and lube."

Ready to Ride

DUANE WILLIAMS

Larry, my buddy who lives down the road, asked me if I might need an extra hand around the farm. He said his nephew was staying with him for the summer, something about a problem between the nephew and his father, Larry's brother. I didn't ask too many questions and, to be perfectly honest, I wasn't too keen about the idea. But I changed my mind when I got a look at his nephew's ass.

He dropped by in the morning after breakfast to introduce himself. I stood on the back porch, watching him come up the lane on a bike. It was another sweltering morning, the air thick with humidity. Larry's nephew wasn't wearing a shirt and, as he got closer, I was thinking that this might just work out after all.

His name was Jason. He said he was 19, although he looked younger. The guy was definitely a looker and well-built for a kid. He had big, solid arms and shoulders. We stood on the back

porch for a while, shooting the breeze about any old thing, mostly about life in the country. He said he loved the country and
had always wanted to live on a farm. He had lots of questions
about why I was out here on the farm by myself. He was from
Toronto, but didn't like the big city and was grateful that his
Uncle Larry was so good to him, giving him a place to stay for
the summer and all. He didn't say too much about his family situation and I didn't ask.

"Looks like you work out," I said, noticing his chiseled pecs
with their fine dusting of blond hair. My dick was noticing, too.
I reached down and gave it a shift.

"Yeah, I guess I've been working out for a few years," he said.

"You look great. You're built like a farm boy."

"Oh, thanks," Jason said, swatting away a fly.

"Damned flies," I said. "Horse flies. They bite worse than
me."

Jason laughed a little and looked away. He wasn't sure how
to take me.

"When would you be ready to start?" I asked.

I'd decided to give him a job the minute I saw him coming
up the lane. I didn't really need any help around the farm, but
it'd been a while since I'd enjoyed the company of a man's ass,
and lately I was boned all the time, sex not being exactly plenti-
ful out here in the country. If nothing else, the kid would do for
some good whack-off fantasies.

"Any time you want me," Jason answered.

"The sooner, the better," I said. "I have lots of jobs that need
doing. But farm work's pretty tough, you know. Sure you can
handle it?"

Jason smiled and nodded. He was getting cuter every minute. My dick was pushing hard to get out, and I gave it a fairly obvious squeeze. Jason noticed. He was trying to look at something else, but I could see he was checking out my package. We made a quick plan for tomorrow and said good-bye. He jumped on his bike and rode fast down the lane, standing up on the pedals. I checked out the incredible ass on that boy. When he reached the road, he looked back at me. He waved and I waved back.

The next morning, he arrived at six, like I'd told him to. We met out back and headed into the barn. Jason had never milked a cow before so I had to show him the ropes. He took to it like he'd been raised on a farm. He had no problem handling the cows, including shoveling up the cow shit. He was even stronger than I'd expected, pushing around the bulls like they weighed nothing at all. He took off his T-shirt and I caught a whiff. He was hot and ripe.

The kid was a hard worker, not lazy like some of the other boys I've had working for me. He did everything exactly as he was told and hardly said a word all morning. Not once did he complain about the stifling heat in the barn. I worked close by to make sure he was doing things right. Truth is, I was boned up and couldn't get enough of that ass. Whenever he squatted to plug the milkers on a cow, his pants slid down, his crack sneaking out over the top. His ass was sweaty, soaking a line through his work pants.

While he was squatting under a cow, he asked me to come over and check out her teats. They seem to be bleeding a little, he said. I went over and squatted beside him. I leaned into him to get a better look and our shoulders touched.

"Yeah, she's bleeding, all right," I said. "Happens sometimes from these damned machines." I went and got the bag balm. I squatted next to him as I spread ointment on the cow's teats. Jason was standing, his ass pretty much right in my face, and it took every bit of God-given strength not to drop the bag balm and go to work on that ass instead. He had a full, round ass—a natural beauty. An ass like that had to be hungry for attention.

"Shit, man, you're really sweating," I said as I finished up on the cow's teats. "Am I working you too hard?"

Jason laughed.

"Let's take a break. It's almost lunch time."

We went down to my dusty little office in the barn where I kept track of the business end of things. I turned on the fan and pulled two Cokes out of the fridge. "There, this should cool us down a bit."

We sat there for a minute or two, chugging the Cokes, neither one of us saying a word.

"I don't know about you," I said finally, "but I definitely need to get out of these sweaty clothes. I'm totally soaked!" I went over and shut the office door. I stripped down to my boxers and sat down again with my Coke. Jason looked a little surprised at first, and hesitated for a minute before undoing his fly. I watched him as he stepped out of his work pants. He wasn't wearing underwear, and his dick was already on the swell.

He stood there for a minute, making a show of his body, and I was happy to watch. He looked down at his thick meat and gave it a tug.

"Nice dick," I said. "Turn around so I can see your ass."

He gave me a smirk, then turned around. He stood there

with his hands on his hips. I started cranking my dick but stopped—too close to blowing a load in my boxers. Jason had a small four-leaf clover tattooed on his butt and his ass cheeks were covered in the same fine hair as his chest. The hair caught the light that was coming in from the window, so it looked golden. I got up off my chair and stood behind him.

"You ever done this before?"

He said no, but I'm pretty sure he was pulling the wool.

I nudged him on the back and he leaned forward against the fridge. He reached behind and opened his ass so I could get a good look at the prize. The hair around his hole was dark and damp.

"Fucking beautiful ass, man."

I dove right in with my tongue. It'd been a while since I tasted ass and his was good and raunchy. He was pushing back into my face, moving his hips around like his ass was on fire.

"Oh ... that feels amazing," he said. I reached through his legs and squeezed his nuts.

I was a hungry man. I kept on eating. Jason groaned like he was about to split in two. Out in the barn, one of the cows in heat was bawling up a storm. It was like she was calling back to Jason, who was just as hot and bothered. I pulled apart his cheeks and started working his hole, circling it with my finger. He was burning up, sweat rolling into the crack of his ass.

"Try going inside," he said.

I tried one finger, then two. On two, he gasped a little. I grabbed the lotion that was sitting on my desk and tried again.

"Oh, shit. Yeah ... that feels great," he said. He was whacking his dick now.

The kid was ready to ride, his body shuddering as I fucked his tight hole with my fingers. I put in a third and he started getting louder than the cow. Between him and the cow, I almost didn't hear Larry's truck coming up the lane. I pulled out, but Jason was on the brink and blew his load on the floor.

When Larry came in the barn, we were dressed and sitting in the office. I wondered if he could smell jizz in the air because he gave me a strange look. Jason was sitting by the fan in his pants and no shirt, flushed, finishing his Coke.

"Just dropped by to see how you boys are making out?" Larry looked at Jason. "Quite a hot one for your first day on the job."

"Yeah, it gets really hot in the barn," said Jason. "It's hard work, but I'm enjoying it so far."

"He's doing a great job, Larry," I added.

Larry looked at me. He hung around for a few minutes to shoot the breeze and then went on his way into town. As his pick-up was going down the lane, Jason and I were already back to tending the cows. The kid didn't say a word for the rest of the day. He was serious and worked even harder than he did in the morning. His pants were soaked right through. When the milking was done and the cows were back in pasture, I showed him the clean-up procedures and we called it a day.

"You did a great job today," I said, giving him a slap on the back. He smiled at me, a little embarrassed. "Coming back tomorrow?"

"For sure," he said. "If that's okay."

"Got lots more to do around here," I said. "I'll see you at six."

He jumped on his bike and I watched that beautiful ass as he rode down the lane, throwing a trail of dust behind him.

Tomorrow's forecast was calling for another hot day in the country.

On Being Single

JOHN DOUGLAS

I've decided to make some changes in my life. Not because of my seroconversion, mind you. That was an effortless event, six years ago, with never an illness worth whining about. Although it does beg the question: if I am undetectable, then why am I so fat? However, I digress.

Following an embarrassing incident at a "gentleman's club," where I inadvertently tried a brand new combination—simultaneously cumming, shitting my pants and spewing fettuccine napoletana all over myself and my anonymous boyfriend in a Linda Blair-ish frenzy—then having to skulk home, covered in alien afterbirth and phlegm—I decided to become a recluse.

I began to haunt gay chat rooms on the Internet. The best part about chat rooms is that you can be anyone: a 70-year-old polio victim confined to an iron-lung and restricted to rasping through a voice box; a crippled dwarf, typing on the computer

keyboard with an insulated hook; Hillary Clinton looking for
Bill; Bill not looking for Hillary.

One afternoon in a chat room, I decided to describe myself
as I really am: mid-30s, HIV+, good looking, with a dick needing action. Response was rapid.

His description of himself was sexy: 30s, fit, also HIV+,
firm buns, into toys. I'm into toys. I have a selection of dildos
that boggles the imagination.

Having established that we liked each other's stats and sta-
tus, we edged round to more pertinent stuff, like where we both
lived. I gave my potential fuck buddy my phone number.
Quicker than you can say "Jackie Collins is a sad old bag," the
phone rang. We arranged to get together, his place, next afternoon, which is now.

I'm looking good. I'd even put on extra teeth whitener
before my Valium last night. It's time to go, so I pack a bag of dildos—just 17 of my favourites—and my afternoon pills, just in
case this turns out to be love.

Halfway to paradise, I pass an old trout in a motorised
wheelchair creaking along at a land-speed-record-shattering
velocity. It's pleasing to see that this respectable senior citizen
has wisely confined herself in her chair. (I hate it when old people fall and break their hips on the footpath where I'm about to
walk.) She's singing to herself. As I overtake the old dear, I can
make out her gnarly lips croaking, "Tonight I'm going to party
like it's 1929 …" I barely manage to resist the impulse to ask,
"Going my way, sister?"

Arrive at my destination. Knock confidently on the weath-
er-beaten door. It opens quickly and there he is. He looks like

Ricky Martin after a nasty battery acid accident. He smiles and he shouldn't have. Teeth that only Helen Keller would have loved. An upper lip in search of a lower to commiserate with. Nostrils? More like collapsing mine shafts awaiting urgent evacuation. A luxuriant crop of blackheads threaten vigorously from the cusp of his chin.

"Baaaaaaaaa."

"I beg your pardon?" I manage to splutter.

"Hi! Come on in."

Before I know it, I'm led inside and despite slipping into shock, I notice he has a fantastic body. Even so, I mentally spank myself for not being more skillful at the chat line thing. Still, I'm here now—may as well see it out. Or in, if he can just hide that face and put his backside in the air.

Tony, as he identifies himself, ushers me briskly through the lounge room. Despite the hurried approach, I do get time to spot some odd things, like a row of mutilated teddy bears sitting in military formation. A poster is taped to the wall on each side of the single window. On the right is Macaulay Culkin. One of the Baldwin brothers is on the left—the ugly, untalented one whose name nobody remembers.

We enter his bedroom. There's rubbish strewn everywhere. Blood-curdling childlike scrawls in crayon virtually obliterate the walls. A Julie Andrews doll wearing a muzzle is nailed to the back of the door. (No need for a muzzle now.)

"Sorry 'bout the mess." He grins sheepishly. Or, at least how a sheep would look if it had clear-lacquered its jaw into a re-enactment of the Challenger disaster.

I tell him to undress. He takes off his clothes and bends over.

There's no denying it, he does have a luscious looking butt, so I think: *Aha, toy boy, let's play!*

I lie him tenderly down on his back on the bed, put his legs over my shoulders and gently stroke around his gorgeous puckered slit. It quivers a little. Just the right amount. Almost a cheeky little wink at me. I tickle and tease it. I spit on a finger and slide it along the soft inner edge of his anus, stopping every so often to rest my fingertips on the outer lips of his sphincter, giving his fuck hole a taste of what's to come. Making it mine.

While my right hand is busy caressing his crack, I use my left to pull a couple of dildos out of my bag. One is a petite and popular 8-incher, the other is a stylish and sophisticated 10-incher. I ask him to choose.

"Oh my god, I can't take that! Or that! I haven't been fucked in two years!"

Loser amateur, I think to myself.

"That's ok," I say aloud.

I dig out some smaller knickknacks—*beginner* anal balls on a string and an anal wand that has small nodules all the way down it.

I lube up the wand and slide it around just outside his butt hole, letting his ass become excited by the pressure of the bumpy rubber prick. He really does have a pretty rear view, I'll give him that. Praise the Lord that he has *something* to make up for that hideous Halloween mask.

By now, his eyes are closed and the look on his face suggests he is either in bliss or his head is collapsing. I insert the lumpy staff into him. One bud pushes past his outer ring of muscle. There's quite a bit of resistance. It takes a determined, steady push to get the thing going into his backside. He wasn't joking when he said he hadn't had anything up there in a while!

Eventually he opens up and swallows the first section of the dildo. I corkscrew the rod even farther up. Each little bump entering causes a small gasp of contentment to escape from his mouth. I don't dare look up to see what I expect is an expression of ecstasy; I don't want to be frightened. I continue until five nodules of the rod are encased in his rectum—mustn't push too far too fast. He looks perfect with a stake protruding from his asshole.

I twirl the slippery butt-stick around, loosening up his hole, freeing it up a bit more. I can feel the inner sphincter in his guts pressing against the end of the love toy, but I can't deep-play with this boy.

I chance it. He appears so peaceful, lying back, giving up his bum for me—this boy with the face of a gargoyle looking upon the kingdom of heaven and hoping that once within there will be no mirrors. Seeing that thing slide even that small distance up his ass is a real turn-on. Despite my best efforts at self-control, and faced with a mush that only a mother baboon could love, I can feel my dick straining and throbbing in my jeans. I work his beautiful, welcoming orifice for several more minutes, let him relax and get used to feeling entered. I am benevolently coring his guts like he's an apple.

But time is passing, and I wanna get something else up there. I also want to finish up and get home in time to watch *Out of the Wok & Into the Closet*, a new sitcom, starring Richard Gere and the Dalai Lama as two fun-loving bachelors sharing a flat in L.A.

Slowly, seductively, I remove the noduled rod. It's time to show this man's rump the variety of feelings it is meant to enjoy. The last rubber bud pops out and his anus closes gently back, but not as tight as it was before, allowing a long-dead-but-still-rotting-road-kill fart to escape.

Phew!

Please, God, help me! I'm gagging, can't breathe! Visions of my last sex and vomit experience flash before my eyes and it takes all my willpower to hold onto my guts. I am not going to puke here in this room.

I struggle to the door and fling it open. Waiting on the other side are an aging couple with Down's Syndrome. It's Tony's parents. His mother grabs the sex toy out my hands. I try to snatch it back, but the greasiness works in her favour. His mother wins the contest, shrieks and runs into to the lounge room, brandishing the slick anal wand like she's a witch. Tony runs after his mother but is no match for her and she proves incredibly adapt at avoiding capture.

Tony is adding a James Bond-ish twist to the scenario by squirting molten Crisco from his ass as we race to catch his elusive mother. The father stands in a corner beating his head. The mother makes a wrong turn and in her excitement skids into her son's bedroom. She's trapped. I walk up to her to demand my dildo back, but there is no need. As my mouth opens to speak, she deftly inserts the greasy wand into my gob and skips out of the room.

Later, I stagger home like a slut who's been fucked ten times bareback by Mister Ed. I've forgotten to take my pills, my legs are aching from the marathon and my clothes are clinging to me with the paste of bum mucus and lube. Somewhere I can hear an old woman croaking, "1929 …" My life is messier than Jocelyne Wildenstein's surgery.

Maybe it's time to look for a steady relationship.

Park Bootie Boyz

JACK R. MILLER

The green, the trails, the dirt, the humidity, the birds, the bees, the trees and the park bootie. Yes, it *can* be found in many suburban, urban and country towns throughout the U. S of A. Many large cities have boyz that enjoy the outdoors, and park bootie comes in many sizes, shapes, tones and sexualities. The park bootie I enjoy most is chocolate and cream. You guessed it: black and Latino bootie gets my blood warm and my cum-juices flowing on high.

I remember one particularly steamy and humid night in an urban city in America. It was hot, still around 90 degrees, perfect park bootie-banging weather. Queenbee was his name. He was very horny and paced his apartment, his hole ready and dripping with excitement for what a park banging would do for him.

Queenbee decided to walk up to the park which was 15 minutes from his apartment. The woods were already full of boyz. The trails were full of old condoms. The trees were shaking with bootie. The gayz, thugz, the trade—all of 'em were lined up, waiting to feel, fuck, slap and eat out a good bootie.

Queenbee saw one tall-ass brother with a foot-long dick. He was leaning against a tree, getting it done with a hot muscular man who was on his knees, deep-throating all twelve inches. What a sight! Farther along, in a little clearing, another dark chocolate thug gave a park catcall for the boyz to come over. Queenbee, Ant-knee and JayZee answered the call, getting there in perfect unison. The boyz began feeling, touching, sucking, and, you guessed it, bootie-banging. Ant-knee was like, "suck on my nutz, yo!" The thug JayZee was like, "slap my azz, toss some salad, yo!"

Queenbee was made to obey. Then they flipped him over and banged the bootie out. One, two, all three of 'em hit that light brown, hairy, deep bootie-hole. The thug boyz banged him until sunset.

Park bootie is best: you don't have to pay for it or marry it. Just slap on a condom, walk the trails and get it done, baby. Park bootie comes in light brown skin, cream colored, dark chocolate, high yellow, vanilla and definitely muscular.

During the summer nights, many boyz are up in those trees wearing clothes that are unclockable by park police. During the summer daze, boyz sit on the benches, thinking about the cum that be flying north, south, east, west, all over the ground. The boyz be thinking about the bootie-holes they'll be climbing up into once the sun goes down. Later on, the sounds of oohs and aahs be swirling in the hot night wind all night long.

Well, my fellow park bootie boyz, be careful, play safe and

always bang that park bootie right into the sunlight when it comes your way. Peace! See ya in da park!

Gym Butt

GYM RATT

Typical morning. I got up, went to the gym, ran, lifted. As usual, after my last crunch, I headed for the locker room. The gym was populated by the same sea of gray hairs I see every morning. Nothing to hold my interest. My timing at this hole in the wall stinks, but it's cheap and near home and work, so I put up with it. Sweaty, flaccid and a little sore, I undressed and walked toward the bathroom and showers.

And there it was. The perfect ass, wearing bright white bikini briefs made even whiter by dark, tanned skin. It was leaning over the sink in the shaving area, owned by a beefy muscle guy with pecs so big, you could stand under them. His skin was perfectly tanned and smooth. He was shaving, inches away from the mirror, and his perfect, round muscle ass jutted out, flexing even.

I hung up my towel in the drying off area where I got an unobstructed view of this massive muscle butt. It was amazing.

The guy remained bent over for days, his briefs straining to cover his ass, cupping his glutes like a second layer of skin. He shifted his weight and a very lucky section of his underwear lodged itself into his crack. My penis was on its way to becoming anything but flaccid. It was time for a very cold shower.

I washed up as fast as I could, but when I finished, the beefy muscle stud and his ass were gone. Disappointed, I dressed and returned to the shaving area to finish getting ready for work.

And there it was again, still only clad in stark white briefs. Its owner had come back to the mirrors, dropped his bag on the floor and bent over to retrieve what turned out to be a bottle of lotion. Slowly, he rubbed it over his smooth skin, his shoulders, the small of his back, his washboard abs. Then he yanked his briefs halfway down his thighs, revealing trimmed pubes and shaved balls. The head of his dick hung flush against his body, but was dark and meaty. While his ass cheeks were tanned and smooth, a black patch of coarse hair ran down his crack. I was transfixed. It was work concentrating on what I was doing—oh, yea, brushing my teeth.

The beefy muscle stud applied a generous helping of lotion to his groin area and proudly rubbed it in. Then he turned away from me and bent all the way over, his head inches away from his shins. The hair in his ass was a treasure trail, leading from the top of his crack to a taunt pink hole, visible because his massive cheeks parted naturally like the Red Sea. He flexed his glutes as he spread lotion on his calves and feet. Then he smeared the white cream all over his ass and gave his huge muscle butt a firm but gentle massage. The guy was making love to his own ass with his hands, not stopping until the lotion disappeared. While he did, I brushed my tongue, imaging it gliding up and down his crack, then swirling around his hot hole. I was completely hard now, and since I didn't wear underwear, my erection was pretty obvious through my tight gray slacks. Fuck it. He was giving me a show and I was displaying my appreciation.

Sadly though, the performance had to end. Without ever acknowledging my presence, he finished up and disappeared into the locker room. I could have used another cold shower but left for work instead.

My timing is perfect now. Every morning, I get up, head for the gym, run, lift. After my last crunch, I head for the locker room. I go into the shower staring at that perfect ass bent over the sink, tight briefs scrunched up between the cheeks, and I come out of the shower, staring at that perfect ass bent over, receiving its daily dose of tender loving care.

Now if I could only work up the courage to offer him a hand.

Rimming a Stranger

IAN PARQUES

For me, the whole point of going to a sex club is to lick some guy's arse crack. I adore rimming, but the added thrill of sticking my tongue into a total stranger's hole is even more exciting. I am always on the lookout for a nice butt to lick and I'm not fussy about the guy's looks, although, of course, being attractive can't hurt. But it's the puckered hole that's most important. My favourite sex club is Power Exchange in San Francisco, which I always visit on holiday. Although the policy seems to encourage the use of dental dams, most guys are happy to have a raw tongue probing deep inside them.

Things were a little quiet the last time I was there, but I still enjoyed looking at the other men getting off with one another, at the occasional cock shoved through a glory hole and the porno movies on the monitors. No one showed any interest in me and I thought this might be my first time *not* scoring in a sex club. But just as I was deciding whether or not to leave, I spotted a guy dressed in a suit and tie, looking like he dropped into the club straight from work. He was around forty years old and smelled pleasantly of alcohol. His hair was dark as were his eyes, and he was clean shaven, although there was a bit of stubble on his chin. Not handsome but very sexy. He wandered around the club with a raging horniness in his eyes, peering into the cubicles, stopping to look at the porn flicks and watching the live action around him. I was determined to have some sort of scene with him.

At one point, he went into the glory hole section of the club, but before I could reach him, someone else got there first. I couldn't even see what my man's dick looked like as it had already found its way down the other guy's throat. I watched for a little while, then went in search of other action.

When I returned to the glory holes, he was gone. I decided to have one last walk around and it was then that I literally bumped into him in the maze. His trouser zip was still undone and his shirt was hanging out at the back, the top button undone and his tie hanging lose—all adding to his raging horny image. He continued walking and I followed him through the maze, cornering him as he ran into a dead-end.

We both smiled and moved toward one another. Within seconds our hands were fumbling each other's pricks. I was greeted by a beautifully-shaped, large, cut dick with a shiny purple head, already dribbling pre-cum. I put my fingers round it and moved them slowly up and down, then pulled his balls through and was pleased to see that they were large, loose, and shaved—just as I like them. He was not gentle with my dick, wanking me hard and fast. It's always been a real turn on to have my prick treated rough and my balls slapped around. All I needed now was to get to that sweet arse opening.

We dropped our trousers to our ankles. He went down on me and sucked hard. His mouth was hot and warm. My dick is a good size, but he swallowed it whole without any trouble and I could feel his breath on my balls. After several minutes, he pulled away and I returned the favour, almost losing my load. His cock and balls smelt of sweat and stale piss. The little bit of unshaved pubic hair above his prick reeked of urine. He obviously wasn't concerned with shaking the last drops of urine from his impressive dick. It was a mega turn on; he was some horny fuck! That arse was going to be mine. I was sure he wouldn't object.

"Can I lick your arse?"

"What?" he slurred, pulling away. Fuck. Perhaps I'd misjudged him, or was it just my English accent he didn't understand?

"Can I lick your hole?"

"Really?" He seemed a bit surprised. "Sure, if you want. It's a long time since anyone has explored there."

He turned around and for the first time, I got a look at his butt. It was firm and well-shaped. My breath was short and fast; I needed to get closer. I went down on my knees, my face inches away from my goal. I placed my hands on his arse cheeks and gently pulled them apart. There it was, that wonderful puckered hole. It was darker than the rest of his butt, slightly hairy and already wet with sweat. That intoxicating man's aroma hit me and I was in. My tongue touched the hole and it reacted immediately. I didn't want to go straight in, deciding instead to savour the joy. I licked up and down and on either side of the hole. My friend was groaning with pleasure. He had definitely been this way before.

Breathing in the smell of his arse, my tongue licking the now-matted wet hairs, I felt light-headed with excitement. My tongue pressed against his shit hole. The tip slid into the entrance and with mutual satisfaction, we both sighed with pleasure. I twisted my tongue into his arse, feeling the sensation as it rubbed the sides of his shit canal and I pushed deeper. He stopped wanking himself and pulled his arse cheeks farther apart so that I could go deeper. I was grateful for the help. My nose was pressed into his arse, my tongue was stretched to its limits. But I needed to go deeper. The taste, the smell, the sensation were all unbelievable, a feeling that makes me higher than any drug could ever. Quite a crowd gathered to watch—probably because of his groaning—and eight or nine guys all had their dicks in their hands, enjoying the floor show. We changed positions: me lying on the floor and him sitting on my face, allowing me even more access to his hole.

My only complaints were that there wasn't enough light to have a good look at his beautiful crack, and that I couldn't see this horny scene like the guys watching could. It must have looked great, this attractive man straight from the office, still wearing his suit jacket with his shirt and tie open, his trousers around his feet, jerking his big dick while sitting on some guy's face.

I licked and lapped at that hole for more than 20 minutes and could have gone on for much longer, but my suited friend came with much noise and mess all over his jacket. I hadn't cum but wasn't too bothered. I would have happily gone back to my hotel with the smell and taste of arsé on my tongue and under my nose and had a really hard wank. No matter how much you rinse your mouth, the taste and smell of a man's hole remains with you—a reminder of that place supposedly out of bounds—and I could have easily taken this man's smell and my hard cock back to my hotel.

But as soon as my friend got off my face, one of the guys watching took his place. I wasn't expecting this but didn't protest. I don't know what he looked like as he moved very swiftly to squat on my mouth. I do know that his hole was shaved and tighter than the guy in the suit. Given a choice, I prefer a little bit of arse hair, but this hole still tasted good. His butt was also bigger, so I had to do a lot of shifting about in order not to suffocate. But it didn't take long before my tongue teased its way inside his hole and I was back in seventh heaven. Five minutes later, the man got up and left, and yes, you guessed it, someone else immediately took his place. Apart from the fact that my body was getting a little stiff and my jaw was aching, I was having a great time, a fantasy come true.

This guy's hole was very hairy and not as clean as the other two, but hell, I was having such a sexy time, the thought that he wasn't very clean made me even hornier. I wouldn't have cared if his butt had been smeared with shit. I needed to make contact with that hole. The taste was a bit stronger than usual, but the smell was just as intoxicating. My prick throbbed away with pleasure and if touched, would have surely shot its load.

At that moment, my racing mind told me that I could get

into scat, but having tried it since then, I know it isn't for me. I'll stick to rimming, whether the butt is clean, smelly or slightly dirty; but I'll leave the messy stuff to others. The third guy came with a tightening of his arse muscles around my tongue and at that point, I almost came as well. But I managed to hold off just in case there were any other interested parties watching. Unfortunately, when the last guy got off my face, all the other guys left the cubicle and I was left lying on the floor, arse hairs in my mouth, stinking of butt, with a raging hard on and a huge grin on my face.

The Forth Bridge

JAMIE ANDERSON

I'm back in my native Scotland for the first time in years. My God, the changes that have taken place. I flew into Edinburgh Airport—no longer called Turnhouse—caught the bus to Princes Street and here I am at what was once the North British Hotel and is now the Balmoral. I wonder if the clock on the tower, high above the hotel, still runs two minutes fast, supposedly to help the passengers catch their trains. Way back then, when I lived in Scotland, it was a soot-blackened building, once described as the ugliest hotel building in Europe. Now they have cleaned it up and it looks a lot better.

I see the old Waverly Market has been changed into a shopping mall. Yes, everything has changed. Even the Waverly steps seem to have become more lethal in a high wind. I carefully hold on to the handrail with my free hand and, carrying my suitcase in the other, descend into Waverly Station. This is the same route that I used to take as a wee laddie to get to and from school. Then I used to fly down the steps, taking them two at a time. I'm lucky I never broke my young neck. God, even the station is different. Half the platforms are gone and it smells different. I get my ticket and go to board my train to Fife. No one even checks my ticket; I just walk onto the platform and board the train! The train is different too, a multiple unit diesel. I get settled down in a corner seat to slowly drift off and remember what it used to be like, way back, when Jock and I played "the game."

It was very exciting as we never knew whether we would get to play it or not. We both lived in Fife and went to school in Edinburgh. This meant crossing the Firth of Forth twice daily. The only methods of crossing then were the ferry boats at the Queensferry passage or taking the train across the Forth Bridge. The bridge is massive and Victorian. Brick viaducts at each end lead out to the three massive cantilevers that span the Firth, and that was where our little game was played.

No modern diesels either. All we had was an old steam train and that was the fun bit. The rolling stock was old and did not have corridors. Each carriage was made up of a series of compartments of eight seats, four facing the engine and four with their backs to it. To play our game we needed a compartment all to ourselves. This was the thrill of it all. We could start out with other people in it, but they might get off at Haymarket or Dalmeny. On the other hand, we might set off alone and someone would board before we got to the bridge. But I reckon about once a week we would be the only passengers in the compartment just before it approached the bridge. Once we went nearly three weeks without playing, while another time we managed it three days in a row.

As soon as the train left Dalmeny Station the game would begin. I liked it in the summer best, because then Jock would let down the window that was set in the door and lean out of it, waving to the people sitting in their back gardens having a cup of tea. They saw a young laddie waving innocently. The picture from my side was a bit different. His pants and underwear were on the floor, his shirt was tucked up at the back and his tight wee bum would be pushed out teasingly in my direction. We had only a wee while to play our little game and, as the wheezing steam engine laboured up the incline to get to the bridge, I would get on my knees behind Jock and part his buns. While he waved to the people, I slowly ran my tongue between his buns, then parted them and kissed his ring. I loved forcing my tongue into him and listening to his moans. Then I'd quickly finger him to get some spit in—our only form of lubricant. By now the train would be steaming along level track before the viaduct and it was time to get my cock out of my pants and into his butt.

To this day I can remember the feeling of entering him. His ring would pull back my foreskin as I pushed my way in, allowing the head of my cock to rub against the warm smoothness of his insides. By then we would be on the viaduct, way below us was the queue of cars waiting for the ferry. We would both wave to the people below; little did they know what we were up to. Then on to the cantilever sections! Here the train made a hell of a noise as it bucked and swayed, making the whole bridge boom like a gigantic drum. Getting a firm grip on his hips, I would fuck him. He would scream for me to do it harder, but I wouldn't. Ah, the feeling of those firm young buns pressed into my crotch. It was heaven.

As we moved from the first cantilever to the second, I would lengthen my stroke, but not enough to end things prematurely. On the third and final one I would really go all out, my hips ramming my cock through his ass cheeks. Jock, now getting fucked as hard as he wanted, would quickly jack himself off, spraying his cum all down the inside of the door and wriggling about on my cock. Seconds later, my balls would be emptied, their contents pumped into his butt.

We would quickly clean ourselves up with our hankies and get dressed. For the short run into Inverkeithing, where I lived, I would lie full length on one of the seats while Jock lay on top of me. As we cuddled, I would slide my hand down the inside of his underwear and fondle his buns. Then I'd slip a finger into his ring and feel the sloppy mess I'd left inside him. As the train slowed for the station we would get ready to leave. He never continued his journey to Aberdour in the same compartment we had used for sex. I often wondered what the next occupants thought of a railway carriage with a cum-stained door and the stink of wee laddies fucking. He would get into another compartment and I'd show my season ticket to the ticket collector, then race up the slope to the bridge that took the road over the line. Once there, I would stand and wave to him until the train chuffed off, round the corner and out of sight. The thought that my cum was riding on the train inside his butt used to give me a thrill. He told me that he tried to keep it inside him as long as possible, at least until bedtime ...

The little diesel is pulling into Inverkeithing station now. There is no ticket collector; I really don't know why I bothered to buy a ticket. The slope seems to be steeper than I remember and, as I slowly climb it, all the other passengers pass me. I'm getting a bit short of breath these days and the suitcase doesn't help, so I pause and watch the train pull out. A wee laddie is waving to someone on the bridge. I spin round and see another laddie waving back. He notices me and we make eye contact. Oh my God, I can see right down into his very soul! The pair of them have been playing our game, but how? The diesel had open carriages, not closed compartments. Wait a minute, of course! The one thing our old non-corridor train never had, a toilet! I smile knowingly at him and get a lopsided smile in return just before he dashes off.

Some things, it would appear, never change.

Fat Butt Greene

GREYSON B. MOORE

"Why do they call you Fat Butt Greene?"

The inquiry came from Alonzo, who sat behind Michael in 8th Grade English. Astonished, Michael scooted up in his seat so his butt wouldn't stick out so much between the steel rods that connected the seat to the back of the chair. But he couldn't stay there for long. His butt kept sliding backward and sticking out as if it were proud of its size. And each time, Alonzo would whisper, "Fat Butt Greene." Michael didn't understand why, but knowing a good-looking male was looking at his rump excited him.

Michael knew his butt was big but didn't think it was fat until that moment in 8th grade. Eventually, he took up weightlifting in the hopes of losing some weight in his ass, but the globes just kept on growing. By the time he finished high school, his backside consisted of two perfectly-shaped ovals with two incredibly deep dimples. His crack was almost imperceptible because of the tightness of his muscled buns.

Diploma in hand, Michael took a job at the local car wash until he figured out what he was going to do with his the rest of his life. He tolerated the job but hated the coveralls and rubber boots he had to wear. The coveralls were made of a white synthetic knit and were very uncomfortable. The owner said the white was to show how neat and tidy his workers were.

One of Michael's fellow workers was a 60-year-old man who the other workers called Gorgeous George behind his back. Michael felt sorry for Gorgeous George because he was anything but gorgeous. Truth be told, he had a face only a mother could love.

One day, when business was slow because of rain, everyone but Michael, George and a cashier were sent home. Michael was happy when a camper pulled in because he figured that would keep him and George busy and the day would move a little quicker. While they were washing the camper, George spilled a whole bucket of water down Michael's back as a prank, only it was no joke to Michael, who yelled furiously when he felt the icy cold water.

"I'm sorry," said George. "I got a towel I can dry you with."

"I can do it myself," snapped Michael.

"Please, let me," George said. His tone was so pathetic, Michael agreed. George started on Michael's back, but quickly made his way to Michael's butt, lingering there for quite some time.

"I think you got it all," Michael finally said.

"I want to be thorough," said George.

Michael felt a warm sensual glow emanating from his buttocks.

"That's enough," he promptly turned to face George. He knew the jockstrap he was wearing would hide what was happening between his legs. He also figured one look at George's ugly mug would kill any hard-on.

Some of the water had splashed on the front of George's coveralls and the white material had become transparent. George was naked under his coveralls and his dick was rigid. Michael couldn't help being drawn to George's crotch.

"Don't you worry about that swelling in your pants," said George. "I like looking at a fine male myself, especially one who has a butt that won't quit." George unzipped his coveralls, letting them fall to the floor. Then he pulled them off so that all that he had on were his boots and socks. "I best hang this up or management will be on my butt. But not like I'd like to be on yours," he said with a wink.

Michael shuddered.

"You might as well do the same," said George. "I could see where the good Lord split you."

Michael backed up.

"Come on baby." George approached. "Make yourself at home."

He grabbed Michael's zipper and pulled it down, then pushed the coveralls down to the ground and pulled them out from under Michael. Now they were both naked except for boots and socks and Michael's jockstrap.

"That's better baby," said George. "Get naked with your

homie. Or is that homo?" He then brandished his meat. "Only decent looking thing on me."

Michael had to agree that old man George's dick was a thing of beauty. It was cut but not visibly scarred. The dark purple head glistened. The shaft was rock hard and sticking straight out without a single vein.

"I've showed you mine, why don't you show me your bumpers," said George. "I think they need some detailing."

Michael glared at George.

"I take it you're not gonna let me wash your butt?" George produced a warm and soapy washcloth. Michael hesitated, then turned around and bent over. The thought of having his butt bathed by another man aroused him, even if the man was George.

"Man," said George, "them white straps frame your pretty brown booty so good. A frame for a bull's-eye. Better take it off though 'cause the pouch may restrict you."

"Huh?"

"I know it's rock hard just like mine." George started to remove the jock. "Man, baby, these straps are so tight, I can barely get my fingers under them. But then that butt of yours is so bountiful, it's no wonder. Once I was on it, I wouldn't want to leave either."

After getting rid of the jockstrap, George washed Michael's behind. The warm soapy water felt extremely sensual, so sensual, it was almost torture.

"Man," said George. "Them cheeks must look good in tight whities."

"I haven't worn those for years," said Michael.

"Don't make 'em big enough to fit over your fat butt and

yet stay on your skinny waist, do they? Even if they did, I bet your big ole butt would bust right out of them. Man, I would love to see that."

The washcloth wound up between Michael's tight cheeks.

"Man, it must take a crowbar to pry them things apart," said George.

When the washcloth slid across his anus, Michael jumped. The feeling was incredible, but Michael didn't understand why. He washed there every time he showered, but for some reason, it felt different now.

"Why don't you bend over more so that I can get a better look," George said after rinsing off the soap.

Michael leaned forward, hands touching the floor.

"I never saw a pair so flawless and beautiful before. When the good Lord was passing out backside, you must have gone back for seconds. Shoot, you must have gone back for thirds. That big ole thing don't have no stretch marks either. It was born to grow big and slow so it wouldn't get ugly." George thumped it with his hand. "I think it's perfectly ripe." He let out a loud chuckle. "Now show your buss."

"My what?" asked Michael.

"What is the younger generation coming to? Your butt hole is also called a 'bussy.'"

The idea of displaying his anus bothered Michael. There was something just plain trashy about doing that.

"Don't be modest," said George. "I bet you have a real pretty one."

Michael scoffed.

"I know, I know. To you it has only one purpose, but to

me ..." George's penis twitched and a shiny drop appeared on the head. "I wish I had brought some rubbers, then you would know what it's also good for."

"You wish." Michael suddenly felt mischievous. He pried his cheeks apart, figuring George would be grossed out at the sight of an asshole.

"*Aiight*, bussy supreme!" A small spurt of semen jumped out of George's dick. "Never saw a butt mustache so thick before. Looks great against your smooth cheeks."

Michael was startled. He wondered how many bussies George had seen and to whom they belonged. George went over to a cabinet and found some plastic wrap. He pulled off a big sheet, placed it on Michael's butt and smoothed it out so that it was like a second layer of skin.

"Now don't be afraid." George's tongue prodded at Michael's anus, causing Michael to flinch. "Not trying to put my nasty thing in there, just Frenching you. The plastic makes it safe."

Before he knew it, Michael was squirming with delight as George rimmed him.

"Oh baby." George kissed Michael's rear. "You are so beautiful."

Eventually, he peeled off the plastic and put his face against Michael's buns. The stubble tickled; Michael was amazed. George appeared to be making love to his rear end.

"Smother me with your fat butt." He stuck his head directly into Michael's split. "*Aiight*, I'm nuttin."

Michael felt hot cum streaming down his right leg. Afterwards, George got a soapy washcloth and washed his juice off Michael's leg. Then he got dressed and left Michael alone in the camper—just in case Michael was angry and having regrets. Michael stuffed his erection in his jock with difficulty, then also dressed and went back to work.

When he got home, Michael took off his damp work clothes and threw them in the washer. No one was home and probably wouldn't be for hours. As he made his way upstairs, he caught a glimpse of his bare behind in the hallway mirror. He still couldn't see what George saw in it. He decided to do a closer inspection in his bedroom.

He sat on the foot of the bed in front of the mirror on the closet door. He lifted his legs over his head and saw the thick forest of crack hair that so impressed George. He spread his cheeks farther apart. In the midst of all of the dark brown flesh was a dense patch of shiny black hair. It reminded him of a black steel wool pad. He put his finger on it and explored it. His finger found his puckered anus, his body shuddering from the sensation. He put the finger up to his mouth and spit on it, then put it back on his anus. He pushed gently against the hole. The lips parted; his finger entered. The sensation was incredible. He was astonished to find another source of sexual pleasure within him. It was difficult to get at, but well worth the effort.

"That's the way baby," he moaned. "Get at that fat butt." He thrust his finger in and out. "Bust my cherry, George."

He stopped for a moment, feeling confused, ashamed and guilty. But his prostate gland could not be denied. It ached for further stimulation. Michael had never felt such urgency. He cast all emotion aside and another finger entered his rectum.

"This is for you, George," he said as he shot a warm load of cum.

Ass on My Mind (and Face and Cock and...)

JOE

Ass. Surely one of God's greatest creations. Ass. Oh, the sheer beauty of it. I'm not talking about the gray, four legged, pointed-eared variety. I'm talking masculine human butts. Pink ones. Brown ones. Pale ones. Ones with tan lines. Plump and rounded, firm and dimpled, young and virginal. Oh, how ass fascinates me. How I love to stare and drool over them. I spend hours looking, feeling and worshipping fine ass whenever I can—which is often, since I have my own loving mate, a most amazing young man.

Oh, to slowly and lovingly caress a round, firm butt. Running my hands over the creamy smooth surface, squeezing the mounds softly, feeling them flex and quiver under my touch. To nuzzle close, burying my face in there, licking, kissing, nibbling. Spreading the cheeks and reveling in the most awesome sight of all, the tiny pink pucker, all wrinkled and pouting.

It has become ritual with me now.

I kneel down. My lover shakes and shivers as I run my hands up and down his legs and over his crotch. I bury my face in his groin, inhaling the male musk that all healthy pubes exude. He teeters on his toes, trying to maintain his balance under my erotic onslaught. My hands reach behind to caress and fondle the twin globes of glory.

I lay him on his back on the couch and get between his legs, spreading them wider. Sitting between those splayed thighs, I look up, thrilled at the way he looks—the anticipation, the hunger, the lust burning through. The almost uncontrollable tremble. The hooded eyes, the parted lips, glistening as his tongue wets them.

I lower my gaze back to the ripe pubes and lunge in. I lick and suck his burning cock, soothing the flames with the caress of my moist tongue, withdrawing before it gets too late. I go lower, between the thighs to suck his loaded balls, one at a time, into my adoring mouth. How amazing those ripe, warm nuts feel in my mouth, the accompanying grunts and groans music to my ears. I love to give pleasure. And pleasure I give, as much or more than what I'll get in return. Giving itself is pleasure enough for me and I lavish it on my partner.

I move on, trailing my tongue over the pubic arch, over the flat stomach and onto his heaving chest. I suckle on those dark pink nipples, holding the tiny nubs between my teeth. Meanwhile, my fingers play little games on his stomach, fluttering in ever-widening circles over the goose-bumped flesh, digging into the belly button, wrapping around the towering flesh of taut man meat. I bury my face in the warm pits of his arms, licking and tickling until the soft hair is glistening with saliva.

He's wild now, so back down I go. I open wide and suck in his drooling cock-tip. I love it and as a reward, give him a full taste of my trained throat muscles. But it's still not time to bring him off. Lifting his legs higher and wider, I trail my fluttering tongue over the knotted nut sac and down along the raised ridge leading to a man's most prized possession, his pucker. I pull apart those awesome cheeks and slip my tongue in the deep crevice, searching for that tiny little orifice, that wrinkled mouth, that tiny pink portal to ultimate bliss. As the tip of my tongue stabs it, he hollers, raising his hips even higher ... a sure sign of his complete surrender to Eros!

I pry open his cheeks and peer closer, my breath coming in spurts, my heart thumping wildly. The anal ring seems to wink at me, the twitching lips pouting like a little girl's mouth. I slobber and drool and suck at the pucker as it pushes out in its mindless passion. His anus is a gaping hole now. I slip a gentle finger in and his whole body shudders. The tender inner linings grab at my probing digit. He hisses and growls, his head rolling from side to side as I lick my embedded finger. He yells out for me to take him. Fuck him!

I lead him to the bedroom on shaky knees, kissing and slobbering all the way. I lay him facedown on the bed and climb in, crouching between his thighs, reaching for those mesmerizing globes. Oh, how my heart thumps. The sight of his hulking form, all prone and stretched out before me, always gets to me. The taut, rippling muscles under the unblemished skin. The gradual narrowing of the broad shoulders to the slim waist. And then the sudden yet gentle rise of the full mounds. I fall between the parted legs and pull the firm cheeks apart, staring at the tiny orifice in awe. It never ceases to fascinate and excite me, that gaping, worked-over and ready hole. No matter how often I've seen it, no matter how many times I've taken it. I'm in love, in love with that tiny, pink opening!

I shove my tongue back inside, my fingers quickly joining in. He gurgles for me to continue. I probe deeper in reply, nudging at the swollen gland hidden in the moist folds of his colon, making him grunt. Every now and then I pull back and look at the incredible sight of that tiny slit, see it twitch and pulse, almost desperate, opening up and pushing out before claming shut like a fish gasping for breath on dry land. As if attempting to reach out and grab at my tongue or finger and pull it back in.

If there's one thing I like even better than eating butt, it's plunging deep into its depths with my rock hard penis. I know he is totally primed for my entry. He can't get any more loose or relaxed. He is absolutely ready! And now it's time for the ultimate joy. I love to make love with him face up, enjoying the whole range of emotions on his handsome face. Even better, I love fucking him from behind, covering his back completely as I lie on top of him and slide in while his awesome bubbles crash against my pubes. I love gripping his hair to pull his head back, turning his face sideways and kissing him as I fuck.

I align my cock with the hole I have just worshipped and he lifts his ass off the bed, his way of letting me know he wants it as

much as I do. As his sphincter snaps over my invading cock, I
hear him wail. I sink in slowly, feeling the thin membrane rolling
sensuously over the entire length of my shaft. I give him time to
adjust. His stomach muscles heave and churn, making the intes-
tine pulse and contract. I slide my hands around him, hugging
him closer.

Soon I'm fucking him with a jolting force, jarring his ass
repeatedly, my groin slapping audibly against his upraised ass
cheeks. Over and over, I draw completely out of his reddened ass
slit, then reenter the slippery channel with a violent thrust. His
overworked colon bubbles around my rampaging cock, coating
it with more slime as the intestinal juice rushes in to lubricate the
welcome visitor.

Time ceases to exist. Grunts and whimpers fill the room.
Harsh breathing and pumping blood drowns out all external
sounds. There is only the blinding pleasure of the ultimate coital
fusion, of the union of man and man. Only the sharp, agonizing
ecstasy of each full-length plunge into the wildly churning caul-
dron. Lust rips through my belly and I increase the speed of my
entry and withdrawal, fucking him with shorter, more vicious
stabs that keep over half of my throbbing cock deep inside the
clutching embrace of his burning rectum. I grab a handful of his
hair, pull his head back and let my lips collide with his open, salivating mouth.

I feel as if I'll go out of my mind.

He tears his mouth away and screams, his body convulsing
violently as his cock jerks and erupts in molten fury. As his balls
expel their contents with an ever-increasing ferocity, his ass goes
wild, seemingly ready to rip my cock right off its root! I bring his

face up and glue my mouth to his, ramming in, squeezing that extra millimeter of my turgid flesh into his bucking tail. Biting his lower lips, I shove in one last time, grinding my pubes into his spread bottom before unleashing a torrent of boiling hot cum into the rapacious, gulping chute, filling him with my seed of life.

As the tremors finally subside and his quaking rectum relaxes, he moans softly, his tight sphincter clutching my softening shaft, the ravaged walls pulsing around my still-buried penis. I wait for a long moment before gently pulling out and lying next to him on the wet sheets, exhausted yet happy.

I remain still, catching my breath. Surprisingly, he is rock hard and I feel that I owe him that much as I crawl lower and take him into my mouth. He needs very little stimulation as he arches his body and lets go of his second load down my throat. I reach under and grab the taut muscles of his ass. He tenses up and I'm more than happy to drink his precious offering, gulping down each spurt of his life-giving fluid as it erupts.

He relaxes. I relax. His cock softens. I think about the perfect geometry of the human body and how pleased God must have been when he created the ass. I look at the man by my side, then close my eyes and send a silent "thank you" to the entire universe.

About the Buttmen

RICK L. ALEXANDER ("Once You've Had Black Ass …"), 34, resides in Kokomo, Indiana, with his partner, Allen McDaniel, 38. Rick has two sons and with his partner's, a total of six children. Born and raised in Wabash, Indiana, Rick attended Indiana University, Bloomington, where he graduated in 1989. He and his partner are members of the Indianapolis Men's Chorus and the Midwest Bear Pack.

JAMIE ANDERSON ("The Forth Bridge") is an aging computer engineer who is still young at heart; locked in the same skull as a vivid imagination; and an occasional contributor to the Nifty Archives. Jamie a contributor to the first *Buttmen*.

JONATHAN ASCHE ("Bottom Floor") has published stories in *Mandate, Torso, Inches, In Touch for Men, Playguy* and *Men*. His work also appeared in the anthology *Friction 3: Best Gay Erotic Fiction*. He is currently writing an erotic novel. He lives in Atlanta.

RL BALDWIN ("Miss Eastview High") is originally from North Carolina but currently resides in Atlanta, Georgia. He possesses a strong desire to destroy the stereotypes that divide the gay and straight black communities. He is sure that his upcoming works will create quite a stir on both sides of the issue.

ALAN BELL (editor) took his first editing credit on his junior high school newspaper. Since then, he has edited *Gaysweek,* New York's first lesbian and gay weekly newspaper; *Kujisource,* a black AIDS newsletter; and several magazines for the black lesbian and gay community, most notably *BLK* and *Blackfire.* For six years, he was film critic for the *Los Angeles Sentinel,* a mainstream black weekly. His film criticism has also appeared in the *Los Angeles Times.* He is a graduate of UCLA, the University of the State of New York and is ABD in sociology at New York University. Bell, who likes to *almost* cover his own butt with boxer shorts and baggy jeans, edited the first *Buttmen* anthology.

WES BERLIN ("No Hole Like the Present") has appeared in a number of gay-oriented publications including *Torso* and *Mandate.* He also appeared in *Slow Grind,* an erotic story collection published by Alyson Books (2000). Berlin can be reached by email at Rimshot99@hotmail.com.

RANDY BOYD ("Rimworld") is the author of three novels, *Uprising,* (nominated for two Lambda Literary Awards), *Bridge Across the Ocean* (nominated for one Lambda Literary Award), and his latest work, the suspense thriller *The Devil Inside.* Randy is an avid sportsman, a lifelong buttman and the mayor of Rimworld.

JAMES COPELAND ("Night Patrol") is a 33-year-old truck driver from New Jersey. He does not describe himself as "gay," but rather "homo-masculine." Copeland is currently studying homoerotic behavior in straight men and their apparent need to "bond" with other men. "A man's ass is the very 'seat' (pun intended) of a man's drive," says Copeland. "A man's ass will dictate how he walks down the roads of life." This is his first published work.

DIRTY TRUCKER RANDY ("Thanks, Bob") is the webmaster of dirtytrucker.com and a working truck driver traveling all over the US. He lives in west Texas on the farm that he was born and raised on. Unpublished except for his web work and winning an essay contest in *Trucker News,* he is looking forward to seeing his work in print. Asked why he qualifies to be a butt-man, he grins and says, "I just love the ass of man."

JOHN DOUGLAS ("On Being Single") is an Australian artist/writer. He writes articles on the lives of HIV positive people in rural areas, and exhibits his artwork—and as much else as legally possible—around the world. He owns no dildos, doesn't watch anything to do with Richard Gere or the Dalai Lama, and does hate old people falling and breaking their legs where he is about to walk. His website can viewed at http://geocities.com/JohnDouglas_Art

MARC EADMON ("Getting a Taste") and his fellow "assologists" delight in the study, pursuit, and enjoyment of the black male ass. Having received his fair share of compliments regarding his own posterior, Mr. Eadmon feels qualified to speak on the subject. "The ideal ass is round and firm, and when unveiled, will inspire the viewer to touch, taste and smell the beautiful sight his eyes behold." Eadmon lives in Los Angeles, California.

MICHAEL GOODWIN ("Eternal Shower") created the very first gay newspaper in Los Angeles in 1968. The Jacksonville, Florida native was also involved in the development of GCN-GayCable Network in NewYork in 1983. During his erotic career, he created the first safe sex videos, *The Goodjac Chronicles*; wrote interviews and articles for *Stallion* magazine; produced and directed 16 explicit videos; and is currently "chronicalizing" his experiences written in over 90 personal journals.

GYM RATT ("Gym Butt") is a buttman from Las Vegas who's been actively enjoying male butt for ten years.

JOE ("Ass on My Mind ...") was born, bred and still lives in India (yea, *India*, as in the land of elephants and snake charmers, sages and mysticism). He wrote his first erotic tale (of the gay variety) in mid-2000 AD, and this is his published first work. The story though largely "fiction," is an exact reflection of his passion: the human male ass. Joe regularly contributes to the Nifty Archive (under the name Outlaw). If you like his story he'd absolutely love to hear from you at outlaw@bbboy.com

PHILLIP McKRACK ("Tony's Tasty Tale") can't remember

when he didn't crave the company of other men. In junior high in the '70s, he had a teacher who looked a lot like Burt Reynolds. "He used to come to class wearing super tight jeans that sculpted that super tight little ass of his." McKrack remembers fantasizing about how perfectly furry that ass must have been under those jeans. His email address is: choclitdayton @yahoo.com.

JACK R. MILLER ("Park Bootie Boyz") lives in Maryland where he is pursuing a degree in Human Services. He has been published by the Famous Poet Society, the Sparrowgrass Poetry Forum, the International Library of Poetry and *Manscape* magazine. Miller says he "enjoys the beauty, the feel, the texture, the joy that a butt brings to a same gender loving man like myself." hotbot21217@yahoo.com. His story "Booty on the Men I Love" appeared in the first *Buttmen* under the name The BGM Poet.

GREYSON B. MOORE ("Fat Butt Greene", "Azzpork, the Horny Ghost") feels that most gay erotica emphasizes the black man's reproductive organ as the sole source of his sexual attraction, often exaggerating its size and output in order to further the point. The black man's backside though has often been ignored as a source of arousal and pleasure for both the admirer and the owner. So he has written erotica celebrating the bounty and the beauty of black men's butts.

PETER MORSHEAD ("Stone Cold Steve Austin's Ass") lives in his native Halifax, Nova Scotia, and has been an avid fan of the male butt most of his adult life. "On the street, in the gym, on a university campus, or in the stores, there's lots of opportunities to scope out a great ass." Morshead thinks some of the greatest butts of all time belong to runners, cyclists, gymnasts, body builders and wrestlers. This is his first published story.

JOSE LOUIS MUÑOZ ("Gay Sushi") left Puerto Rico at the age of 18 to look for adventure. New York City was the playground of choice. Then he joined the Marines in what he calls his best acting job. Next, he pursued degrees in Film and Theater with a minor in Italian. He has currently written 15 plays, one book, hundreds of poems, songs, some short stories and an episode for *Law & Order* (currently being considered for production).

IAN PARQUES ("Rimming a Stranger") realized he was gay when he was 12 and had his first sexual experience when he was 14. Today he lives with his partner of three years in his native London and works for an organization that deals with complaints about advertising. His favourite part of a man's body is "that lovely butt hole." He has a number of sexual interests, "but nothing beats rimming." He appeared in the first *Buttmen*.

ROBINMAN ("Bluejay") began writing erotic superhero stories in 1993. His work has been seen on "fan-fiction" or "slash" message boards and sites in various places around the Internet. He is eager to write more costumed capers for the reading public. His story "Redhawk" appeared in the first *Buttmen*.

SIMON SHEPPARD ("The Boy Who Read Bataille") is the author of *Hotter Than Hell and Other Stories* and the co-editor, with M. Christian, of *Rough Stuff* and *Rough Stuff 2*. His work has appeared in over 65 anthologies, including the 1997, 2000, and 2002 editions of *The Best American Erotica,* and nearly every edition of *Best Gay Erotica*, as well as the first *Buttmen*. Visit him at www.simonsheppard.com.

TROY YGNACIO SORIANO ("The Thrill-Seekers Luncheon") lives in Boston, Massachusetts. He is 29 years-old and hard at work on many writing projects, including a novel, a play, and a monthly magazine. He maintains a website at www.troysoriano.com. His story is dedicated to his friend Smash, and to strictly-speaking cowboys across America. His story "America's Passion Kings" appeared in the first *Buttmen*.

JAY STARRE ("Appreciating My Assets") resides in Vancouver, British Columbia, where he pounds out porn at a furious pace. He has written for most gay mags, including *Honcho, Torso, Mandate, International Leatherman, Bear, Indulge* and others. He has also written for nearly a dozen anthologies, including *Friction 4* and the first *Buttmen*. Jay greatly appreciates the male butt in all its forms.

MATTHEW STEWARD ("What Is It About Butt?", "In Praise of Big Black Ass") is a college instructor living in New York City.

TROY STORM ("Butt Brigade," "Getting Behind in Business") has had over two hundred erotic stories published in gay, bi and straight publications. "Best Buddy" appears in the *Men for All Seasons* anthology. His collection of short stories concerning

West Hollywood gym jocks, *Gym Shorts,* is available now from Companion Press. Troy freely admits that the sight of a solidly-constructed butt and the treasure that lies therein makes him really sit up and grab his thesaurus.

M. THOMAS ("Kenny's Ass") is a retired intelligence analyst and attorney. He is an avid buttman and fledgling writer of erotic non-fiction, much of which explores his fascination with the taste, smell and beauty of the male ass. He lives in San Diego, California, with his life partner, with whom he shares his love of photography, movies, cooking, reading, mustachioed men and their asses.

BILLY TWEE ("Comfort Station") writes erotica from his home in San Francisco and may be reached at billytwee@yahoo.com.

DUANE WILLIAMS ("Ready to Ride") lives near Toronto. His fiction has appeared in *Queer View Mirror, Quickies, Contra/Diction* and *Harrington Gay Men's Literary Quarterly.* He is currently at work on a collection of short stories. "Ready to Ride" has given him new *asspirations* in life.

west beach books ● more about buttmen 2 ●
coming up next ● more about the authors ●
for authors ● submission info ● contact west
challenge ● behind the book ● other west
buttmenfunzone.com ● contact the editor ●
write your own review ● reviews ● guidelines
beach books ● ebook info ● celebrity butt
beach books ● more about buttmen 2 ●
coming up next ● more about the authors ●
for authors ● submission info ● contact west
challenge ● behind the book ● other west
● write your **surf's up** own review
● reviews ● guidelines
for authors ● submission info ● contact west
challenge ● behind the book ● more about
west beach books ● contact the editor ● more
reviews ● guidelines for authors ● submission
● celebrity butt challenge ● behind the book ●
buttmen 2 ● buttmenfunzone.com ● contact
authors ● write your own review ● reviews ●
contact west beach books ● ebook info ●
other west beach books ● more about
about the authors ● contact the editor ● write
authors ● submission info ● contact west

buttmenfunzone.com • contact the editor •
write your own review • reviews • guidelines
beach books • ebook info • celebrity butt
beach books • more about buttmen 2 •
coming up next • more about the authors •
for authors • submission info • contact west
challenge • behind the book • other west
buttmenfunzone.com • contact the editor •
write your own review • reviews • guidelines
beach books • ebook info • celebrity butt
beach books • contact the editor • coming up

www.westbeachbooks.com

beach books • ebook info • celebrity butt
buttmen 2 • buttmenfunzone.com • other
about the authors • write your own review •
info • contact west beach books • ebook info
other west beach books • more about
the editor • coming up next • more about the
guidelines for authors • submission info •
celebrity butt challenge • behind the book •
buttmen 2 • buttmenfunzone.com • more
your own review • reviews • guidelines for
beach books • ebook info • behind the book

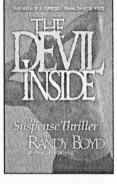

ALSO FROM WEST BEACH BOOKS
More Kick Ass Erotica

32 stories
1 obsession

Buttmen

Erotic Stories and True Confessions
by Gay Men Who Love Booty

Edited by **Alan Bell**

"Nothing short of a sexual thunderclap. Every buttman will close this book with a fresh appreciation of his own fascination for that wonder of creation, those twin mounds of masculinity."
Playguy Magazine

"*Buttmen* turns out to be more than just soft porn fluff. [It offers] entertaining and honest commentary on a fetish close to many men's hearts."
Watermark

"A bootilicious frenzy [full of] explicit, steamy tales."
Eclipse Magazine

"Diversity is what recommends this collection. White men [and] men of color ... come together in these pages to wax rhapsodic over beautiful backsides."
Lambda Book Report

"Almost every conceivable variation on eating and/or probing the human ass is explored in *Buttmen*, at least once."
X-Factor

Buttmen
Erotic Stories and True Confessions by Gay Men Who Love Booty
Edited by Alan Bell

Available at bookstores and on the net
in traditional print and eBook formats

www.westbeachbooks.com
www.buttmenfunzone.com

Printed version ISBN 0966533305
ISBN may vary on eBook editions

Printed in the United States
35036LVS00006B/53